Being a bridesmaid at her best friend's wedding in the sleepy town of Mule Hollow Texas is the perfect place for Amber Rivers to lay low to avoid a stalker hot on her heels back in Houston. She loves her job and her city life and isn't looking to stay long in the country-but she's blindsided by her attraction to the self-assured rancher, Chase Hartley...

Chase agrees to watch over socialite Amber while his partner heads off on his honeymoon but despite the high voltage sparks lighting up between them he has no intention of getting any closer to Amber than necessary to keep her safe. But he soon realizes there's a whole lot more to Amber than he first assumed and keeping his distance is becoming harder with every passing moment they're together.

An outside threat plus a little friendly tampering from the meddling Matchmakin' Posse of Mule Hollow puts this couple on high alert as they try not to fall in love.

Chase

NEW HORIZON RANCH

MULE HOLLOW BOOK 3

DEBRA CLOPTON

ABOUT DEBRA CLOPTON

Bestselling author Debra Clopton has sold over 2.5 million books. Her book OPERATION: MARRIED BY CHRISTMAS has been optioned for an ABC Family Movie. Debra is known for her contemporary, western romances, Texas cowboys and feisty heroines. Sweet romance and humor are always intertwined to make readers smile. A sixth generation Texan she lives with her husband on a ranch deep in the heart of Texas. She loves being contacted by readers.

Visit Debra's Website and sign up for her newsletter for news and a chance to win prizes
http://debraclopton.com

CONTENTS

About Debra Clopton

CHASE

Dear Readers

New Horizon Ranch: Mule Hollow Series

More Books by Debra Clopton

CHAPTER ONE

The cowboy had her attention the moment he rode the golden horse over the hill. The horse galloped at full speed, cutting across the pasture, with the man riding low in the saddle. Man and horse almost one as they charged down the slope then angled along the fence.

Amber Rivers almost ran off the road watching them.

Graceful, masculine...breathtaking.

She had her top down on her convertible and for a moment her car was almost neck and neck with the horse and cowboy. She couldn't help herself when the cowboy looked over his shoulder at her, she laughed...and pressed the accelerator.

The cowboy grinned and urged his horse faster to keep up. She laughed again feeling invigorated by the exchange. The wind stinging her cheeks made it almost feel as if she were riding a horse beside the cowboy. She slowed almost without realizing it so they continued to run parallel to each other for a few yards. The New Horizon Ranch entrance loomed suddenly down the road. She slowed the car then pulled into the drive. The cowboy had slowed his horse to a trot and she pulled the car to a halt in the lane. She watched him ride toward her.

He wore tan chaps with a deep cranberry colored shirt and a pale straw cowboy hat pulled low over his eyes. What a picture he made with the sun beaming bright and seeming to cast a spotlight on the golden horse and its rider.

Amber got out of the car and walked around to the fence as he rode up on the other side. "Hey there," she said. "That horse had some race in him."

Sitting straight in the saddle the rugged cowboy's lips hitched into a proud smile and Amber's stomach dipped.

"Oh yeah, Nugget can hold his own alright. I think you must have a little NASCAR in you."

She laughed and cautiously reached out to pet the horse's forehead. "That's me, a Richard Petty wanna be."

That won her a chuckle and an appreciative

sweep of his gaze. "I bet you'd hold your own out there. Are you Amber? Sadie's friend?"

She met his steel gray eyes and for a minute she forgot everything, even that she was here to be maid of honor in her best friend's wedding. "I am," she said, after a second. "And you are?"

"Chase Hartley, I'm one of the partners who own the ranch. Sadie's up at the house. I won't keep you since I know she's anxious to see you."

"Thank you. That horse is a beauty. I don't think I've ever seen a horse that looks so handsome. I love that golden color."

As if the horse knew he was being talked about he pranced to one side and nodded his head, straining on the bit in its mouth. Chase chuckled. "You'll give him a big head. He gets told he's beautiful all the time, but handsome is good for his ego"

"Then I'm glad I could help his ego." You're not bad yourself she almost said but reined in her tongue before the words came out. "Is the ranch far?" she asked, deciding it was time to turn this conversation back where it was supposed to be. She wasn't here to flirt or think about flirting.

"It's not far and as I said Sadie's at the house waiting on you." He tipped his hat. "I believe I better get back to work. It was nice meeting you, Amber."

"You too. I'll see you later."

"No doubt about that." He smiled again, then with a nudge of his knee the beautiful horse loped away.

Amber watched them go…but it wasn't the horse she was watching.

Not that she was interested in anything that had to do with a cowboy or small towns but wow.

Just wow. "That was some cowboy," she muttered and climbed into the car and drove down the long drive outlined with pipe fence and oak trees.

The house was a towering two story, white sandstone with massive windows and a large terrace starting at the side doors and wrapping around to the rear of the house. The site of the house and that she would soon see Sadie sent relief coursing through Amber.

The yard was shaded by huge oak trees that would offer a reprieve in the summer months from the relentless Texas sun. To Amber the main house of the New Horizon Ranch was a welcomed site. And for a few weeks it would be her reprieve. Her hideaway.

She parked her small sports car in the parking area and slid out of the car and closed the door. She stretched, having driven for nearly four hours with only a few breaks. Sadie's sudden wedding had come at the perfect time for Amber. She'd needed to get away for a little while. Her job at the abuse hotline center exposed her to a lot of stressful situations and sometimes, like now, despite every effort for anonymity she was placed in the direct path of trouble.

She was ready to see and hug her best friend as much for herself as for joy at Sadie's newfound happiness. But this was Sadie's time. Her happy celebration and Amber would push her own problems to the back burner. She was concentrating on Sadie for the next few days.

And not the mess she'd gotten herself into back home in the Houston suburbs.

She leaned into the car and grabbed her purse and her phone and as she started up the flagstone walkway she slung the purse over her shoulder and dropped her phone into the outer pocket. She was almost to the patio when one of the French doors flew open and Sadie rushed outside. "You're here!" the leggy, red headed beauty exclaimed rushing from the house and engulfing Amber in a tight hug that involved rocking from side to side and having the breath squeezed right out of her. Laughing, Amber hugged Sadie just as exuberantly. She had needed this hug more than Sadie would ever know. "It's so good to see you," she said, and meant it.

"You too, my friend." Sadie pulled back but kept her arm around Amber's shoulder. "Come inside. I've got nice cold tea and some cookies—although, I have to admit that though I'm getting better in the kitchen I'm no Betty Crocker. Not even close."

The very idea of her buddy even being near the kitchen made Amber laugh again. "I still can't believe you hired on here as the cook. And that you *like* it."

Sadie's face dipped into a comical expression of confusion. "Go figure. Surprised me too. But believe me I have a long way to go. Thank goodness for the Food Network!"

She dropped her arm and led the way into the kitchen. Amber followed her into the gorgeous room. Amber and Sadie had both seen their fair share of expensive kitchens, so she understood that the previous owner had spared no expense in this room. It was decked out with amazing granite countertops, stunning walnut cabinetry with intricate details and the tiled floors were pure beauty.

"Wow."

"I know, have you ever seen such beautiful woodwork on cabinets? CC who owned the ranch had expensive taste."

"A *yeah ya think!*" Amber teased. "Kind of reminds me of your mother."

"You've got that right. I'm building something more casual than this showplace and it's going to be wonderful but not this amazing. Rafe and I want our place to be comfortable and welcoming and very family friendly. I have no plans to make it extravagant. I can't wait for you to see it."

Amber dropped her purse onto a barstool then leaned against the counter and watched her friend quickly fill two glasses with ice and tea. "You look so happy, Sadie. I mean I knew you sounded happy over the phone but you just beam."

Sadie blushed. "I never thought I could be this happy." She passed a cold glass to Amber then led the way to the table. They settled into the chairs and Sadie sighed.

"Sometimes the worst day of your life can turn into the best day of your life. And that's what happened to me the day I met Rafe."

Sadie had been a week away from her wedding and found her weasel of a fiancé with another woman. Just thinking about it spiked Amber's blood pressure. Sadie had gotten in her car and driven away and then she'd kept on driving. She'd run away and hadn't stopped until she'd broken down here on the outskirts of Mule Hollow, four hours away from home. Rafe had stopped to help her.

"I agree. The day you met Rafe and stopped thinking about that good for nothing weasel ex-fiancé," she halted, having to bite back a foul mood. Just thinking about Sadie finding her ex with another woman sent Amber's temper boiling again. "Okay, I'm going to take a deep breath now and think the good thoughts—"

"Which are me ending up here and meeting Rafe that same day. God took something terrible and made it for good. He's like that you know."

"Oh yes, so true."

They both laughed though they were completely serious in everything they'd said. Amber had never liked the first fiancée and had kept her opinion to herself because she loved Sadie. But Andrew's fooling around hadn't surprised her in the least.

She squeezed Sadie's hand. "I'm so happy for you and can't wait to meet this hunk of burnin' love that swept you off your bunny feet." She smiled at that—Sadie had gone through all of that wearing her big hairy white bunny suit…the one she wore to the cancer center to cheer up sick children. There was no telling what Rafe thought when he'd spied her on the side of the road. Amber would have loved to have been a fly on the window to have seen that.

"Oh, you'll meet him soon. He wants to meet you too. He's in town picking up supplies but will be back to put dinner on the grill. He and all his partners are doing dinner. You're going to love him. You're going to love all of them. They're a great group."

"I already do love him. He loves you and that makes me love him." It was true. Sadie deserved so much love and she looked so very happy. It did her heart good seeing the joy on Sadie's face. Thoughts of Chase Hartley flashed like a neon sign in her mind. "Oh, I've already met one of the partners."

"You did—who?"

"Chase Hartley. He was riding a gorgeous horse up by the road when I reached the entrance. He and the horse kind of raced my car." She laughed.

"And the horse was so amazing I had to stop and look at it."

Sadie eyes lit with mischief. "So, only the horse was gorgeous?"

The handsome, steel blue-eyed cowboy with the dark brown hair filled her mind. "Oh, I cannot tell a lie—the cowboy could turn heads too."

Sadie grunted. "Un-huh got that right. He's a great guy too. I really wanted you to meet him. I've been thinking you two might hit it off."

Amber stared at her friend. "Oh no you don't. You know I don't like the logistics of small towns. They're away from everything. Not to mention, I have my job." Or at least she thought she still had her job. Being forced to take a leave of absence had her on edge. Lately, she was becoming more and more frustrated by certain things. That included having one of the abused victim's violent boyfriend discovering her identity and that she'd talked his girlfriend to go into hiding...*nope, no ma'am you aren't going there. Focusing on Sadie— remember?*

Not her troubles back in Houston. Right.

She shot Sadie a gentle warning. "When I want one, I can find my own boyfriend. I do not need you trying to match me up with your friends."

"But that's just it—you don't date. You're too young to just spend all your time talking to hysterical, fearful, and hurting victims. And when you're not doing that you're teaching women how to hurt men who want to hurt them. There is no normal in your life. You need to get around some good men…because believe it or not they are out there," Sadie pleaded, then her expression turned impish. "Several are right here on this ranch."

Amber took a deep breath. "Okay, girlfriend. I love you dearly and I am overjoyed that you've found your man, but I'm not ready to settle down. Especially in a small town. Besides this is supposed to be all about you right now, not me. This is your wedding we're about to have on Saturday. That's only two days away and I'm focused on that and nothing else. And I might add, so should you be."

A sweet, dreamy look came into Sadie's eyes. "Oh I am focused. I just want you to be as happy as I am. And if you'd just give Mule Hollow a chance it's a wonderful small town. And since you're going to be here for a month…it could happen."

"I'll be coming here to visit because you're my buddy, but I can promise you I'm not falling for a small town. And I will never, ever fall for a

11

cowboy—so give it up girlfriend."

"But—"

"*Sadie.*" Amber laughed and after the day—*the week*—she'd had it felt good. Sadie had no idea that a man for herself was the *last* thing on Amber's mind right now. A vivid image of Chase galloping across the pasture filled her mind in that instant. Okay, so there had been that moment but that was all it was…a moment.

"Fine. For now," Sadie huffed. "But one day I'm going to succeed in helping some wonderful man find you and make all your dreams come true."

"You're impossible," Amber retorted but let the notion sink in…was there such a man out there for her? Had she given up on finding—or even believing a man like that existed? *Especially* for her.

"So, since you're not staying here for a month to see if you'd like to live here, now can you tell me why you're suddenly taking a leave of absence from your job to hang out with me on the ranch for four weeks? Don't get me wrong, I'm thrilled you're here but what's going on?"

The matchmaking attempt Amber hadn't been expecting. But, she'd been waiting for this but hoping she wouldn't ask. "Just…having a bit of trouble with a case I'm involved in. It's nothing to worry about."

"A case?" Sadie asked. "As in an abuse case?" She stiffened in alarm. "Amber, is someone bothering you?"

Amber pushed her shoulders back and ignored the trickle of fear trying to wedge its way into her mind. It wasn't as if she hadn't been in bad situations before and that was exactly what she imagined Sadie was thinking about right now.

"Let's just say I have someone else's angry boyfriend on my hands. He found out where I was and followed me to the grocery store two days ago." She didn't tell her that he'd been following her around or that he'd written threats and placed them in her mailbox.

"You're being stalked?"

"No. Now Sadie, don't make more out of this than there is. I'm here to just make sure I'm safe so please let's not worry about this right now. This weekend is about you. I'm here, I'm safe and by the time I go home this will have calmed down." She really hoped Sadie would stop looking at her like that. She'd always worried about Amber working at the center so this wasn't helping calm that fear. "The guy has no idea I'm here or how to find out where I am. So there's one good thing about this tiny hole-in-the-road town you love." She smiled at her friend she loved so much.

"So, he's trying to find you and that's why you're here for a month—you're hiding out? Oh, Amber, I know you and you're not telling me everything. There's more isn't there?"

Amber sighed, realizing the best thing was to get it out there and then move on so Sadie would concentrate on her wedding. "Okay, he broke into my apartment and the police advised me that getting out of town for a while would be advisable. The hotline center insisted I take a leave of absence just to be safe. Your wedding came at a perfect time. Now, they have it under control and will call me the moment they learn anything else. Please stop worrying about me. You know I can take care of myself."

Sadie didn't look entirely convinced but after a second she smiled back. "Okay, so the good thing is you're here for a month and who knows, you might just decide Mule Hollow's exactly where you need to be."

Amber just shook her head. Sometimes the best thing to do was to say nothing. Because though Sadie obviously had other hopes for her, Amber knew that falling for a small town or a cowboy…just wasn't happening. Besides, she'd never been one to hide from trouble and it felt counter to everything for her to be hiding out.

With the wedding that weekend it had just worked out for the best.

But living here permanently wasn't going to happen.

CHAPTER TWO

Chase rode out toward open pasture and let Nugget gallop, needing to ease the tension coursing through him as much as the recovering horse needed the exercise. Amber Rivers had been something. Small with thick reddish brown hair that sparkled like fire in the sunlight.

He pulled on the reins and slowed the buff gelding to a trot when they reached the hilltop. From that vantage point he watched Amber's cherry red sports car stop at the ranch house in a haze of dust.

She's a socialite.

He'd known Sadie's best friend was coming in from the city for the wedding. He also knew that Sadie came from high society and her friend would be of the same circles. He reminded himself he wasn't interested in society women—not any more. Though Sadie was a great gal and broke the preconceived ideas about high society women that didn't alter the fact that he wasn't lookin' in the society pages for a date...much less a future bride.

The free-spirited way Amber Rivers had raced her car against him and Nugget, her hair flying out behind her in the wind and the impish glint in her eye when she'd brought the car to a gravel spinning halt had taken his breath away.

But that didn't matter. Even if he didn't already know she was from the same social circles as Sadie everything about her said high maintenance. Her sparkling BMW convertible sports car, the jewelry dangling from her ears and wrist winking at him in the sunlight...all of it said she was not his type.

Not anymore anyway.

Been there, done that and learned from the experience with no plans for a repeat.

"Is your mother going to make it to my wedding?" Sadie asked later after she'd given Amber a tour of the house.

"Yes, she wouldn't miss it. And how about your mother?"

"Coming. But heaven help me she's driving me bonkers. I've had to put my foot down several times, and thank you very much for helping me have enough backbone to do that. I love my mom but you know what I'm talking about."

Amber laughed. "Oh believe me I do." It was a known truth that Sadie's mother was a little controlling and over the top on doing things for the sake of appearances. Amber's mother was a caterer and Sadie's mother and her social circle were some of her best clients. Amber had met Sadie when she'd gone to help her mother in the kitchen during one of those events and they'd become friends. Shy Sadie had been drawn to Amber's boldness. Sadie was nothing like her demanding mother.

"When I told her I was having a simple fall wedding in the little church here in Mule Hollow she literally acted as if I'd just torn her heart out. But I held my ground."

Amber was proud of her gentle-hearted friend. This was a big step for her. Running away had been good for her. Rafe had been good for her.

"I do believe you may have finally let your true light out to shine for all of us to see."

Sadie blushed. "I'm more at peace here and more sure of myself here in these surroundings. And I'm having a small wedding in this quaint church with a cowboy preacher preforming the ceremony and that is final. Oh there's Maddie. She's come to meet you before she heads home to get ready for the BBQ tonight."

The glass door to the kitchen opened and a pretty young woman around their age entered. She had a mass of dark curls pulled into a ponytail and wore a hot pink tank top with jeans that were tucked into dust covered cowboy boots.

"Hey there." She greeted them and Sadie made introductions.

Maddie would soon be Sadie's sister-in-law since she was married to Rafe's twin brother, Cliff. But she was also one of the five partners who had inherited the ranch from their former boss. Maddie oozed confidence. Amber had a feeling she knew how to take care of herself too. It was just something Amber noticed about women.

"Maddie's amazing," Sadie bragged. "She can ride a horse like crazy. And you should see her work cattle. She can manhandle those cows like she had the strength of five men."

"Well maybe the strength of three men," Maddie said, her eyes sparkling. "I've heard a lot about you too. Sadie says you'd make a great cowgirl."

19

Amber choked on her tea and looked at her friend in shock. "What? She's kidding."

Sadie shook her head. "I'm not kidding. You've always been a little bit of a western heroine to me the way you always want to make things right when injustice is being done."

"All you need is a horse," Maddie quipped.

"And next I guess you'll say I need a badge," Amber grunted.

Sadie grinned at her. "Nope, just a horse and a cowboy." "You are really pushing it, girlfriend."

Both Maddie and Sadie laughed on that one just as Amber's phone rang. Instantly her stomach clenched as she glanced over at her purse.

"Aren't you going to get that?" Sadie asked.

She eyed her purse. "Nope. It'll go to voice mail. We're visiting right now." She hated this. She wasn't one to get frightened easily but after this last week…this guy had her worried. There was no denying it to herself any longer. "Are you okay? You're pale." Sadie looked at her in alarm.

Thankfully the phone stopped ringing. She was going to have to put it on silence from here on out. If she didn't want to answer her phone, she didn't want to answer questions about why either.

Maddie was studying her. "You are pale. What's

20

wrong?"

"I'm fine. I didn't sleep well last night and after the long drive it's starting to get to me. Nothing to worry about." This was not a lie, she hadn't slept at all last night. "I'll be fine after I get some sleep tonight." She stood. "Now, stop worrying about me and let's go see this house of yours."

CHAPTER THREE

Chase was helping Rafe grill steaks on the patio that evening and their other partners, Ty and Dalton, were all gathered around talking when Amber and Sadie came outside to join them. She wore white shorts an orange top and some strappy sandals. Chase's pulse kick started the moment he spotted her.

"I think you've met Amber," Sadie said to him after she'd introduced Amber to Ty, Dalton and Rafe.

"Nice to meet you again," he said. "Raced any horses lately?"

She laughed. "I haven't had the chance but it was fun while I did."

Ty gave her a grin—and that was saying a lot from the quiet horse trainer. "I could put you on a real horse instead of that toy you call a car sitting out there."

"Now Ty, don't insult the lady's choice of transportation," Chase warned with a chuckle.

Dalton gave a skeptical look toward the car in question. "I'd hate to have to crawl in and out of that tiny thing more than once a month. But then, you're a lot smaller than I am. And look a lot better getting in and out of it."

Chase watched his partners turn on the charm.

She laughed. "Insults will get you nowhere boys. That's my baby out there and I like the way it rides just fine."

"It looked good to me this afternoon," he added picturing the playful gleam in her expression when he'd first looked over and connected with hers. She looked at him now and he felt the pull of attraction once more.

Rafe held out a hand to her and gave her a warm smile. "It's great to finally meet you, Sadie says you are the most amazing person on the planet and has been chomping at the bit for you to get here."

Amber looked skeptical. "And my friend is biased. Ever since we met she's been blinded to my faults because she's too nice to notice them."

"Not true," Sadie said. "Well kind of true. Not long after we met some boys were picking on me at school and Amber stepped in between them and me, despite being a foot shorter than me, than most people, she took up for me. Ended up stomping one boy's foot, kicking another in the knee and giving the meanest one a black eye. And she did it so fast she didn't break a sweat."

Chase wasn't the only one startled by the info. Amber was small, but she was also strong he could tell by the definition of her biceps and in those shorts she had really well defined legs. The lady was in shape and it sounded as though she had always been.

She laughed then and looked a little embarrassed. "They were wimps. And I got a little carried away, because they made me so mad."

"Sounds like you addressed the problem," Dalton drawled, respect in his gaze. Ty nodded agreement.

Chase muttered that he agreed too, wishing he'd spoken sooner, said the words Dalton had said he'd been too surprised by the story.

Rafe pulled Sadie against his side in an affectionate hug and kissed the top of her head. "Thanks for taking up for Sadie. I figured you must be pretty special or Sadie wouldn't think so highly of you."

24

"Like I said, she's biased but so am I. Guess that's what friends do, they overlook faults. So y'all are all partners? Cool."

Chase recognized her smooth change of subject, switching the conversation to them and off of her. Sadie clearly adored her friend but all that praise would have made him itch with uncomfortableness. He didn't blame Amber for wanting to change the subject.

"We overlook each other's faults too," Ty said and gave her a wiry grin.

"Hey, I don't *have* any faults to overlook," Dalton said, winking at Amber.

Rafe chuckled. "And even though we don't always agree on some things…like Dalton's lack of faults—we're making our partnership work by using each other's strengths."

"So true," Sadie agreed. "Each of you has a specialty. Ty with the horse training, Rafe and Dalton with the cattle. Maddie with the motherless calves. And then Chase with the books."

"That's probably part of why your boss chose to leave his prized ranch to all of you. Team work." Amber glanced at him.

"Probably true. But any one of us could have inherited the ranch and had the skill to keep the ranch going…even thriving. CC saw something in each of us that had him placing our names on that deed. And, he liked us."

"True," Ty said, shooting Dalton a skeptical look. "Not exactly sure why—" That got chuckles from everyone.

Dalton gave Ty a humorous scowl then smiled at Amber. "We liked and respected him too."

Everyone agreed with nods or words.

"You must be real special since you're the only person other than her mother that Sadie has invited to the wedding," Chase said, not letting the conversation stray away from her even though he could see that she wanted it to.

"And I still haven't figured out how that happened."

That made Chase smile as he turned to flip steaks. "Rafe, you better call your brother and tell him and Maddie that they need to get a move on or their steaks will be cold."

"No need, there come the love birds now," Dalton said. "I'm not sure we're ever going to get any work done around here with more newlyweds on our hands, they're worthless."

Everyone laughed at that and were still grinning when Maddie and Cliff walked up arm in arm.

"Y'all almost missed the steaks," Chase admonished, taking the tongs and lifting the meat onto the platter beside the grill.

Cliff had his arm draped around Maddie's shoulders. "Hey, you boy's see my wife during the day and I like spending time with her too—so deal with it."

Maddie smiled and kissed him on the cheek. "I agree completely." She looked at Amber. "Sorry we're late. This is my husband, Cliff—Rafe's twin. As you can see they don't look a lot alike."

"I'll be able to tell them apart then." Amber shook Cliff's hand. "It's nice to meet you. I see a resemblance though."

"I'm the sweet one," Cliff teased.

"Subjective—" Rafe grunted as he helped Chase pull steaks off the grill onto the platter.

Chase listened to the exchange then carried the platter over to the patio table and set it down beside the warmer that held the baked potatoes. "Ok everyone, chow time."

Everyone sat down and busied themselves loading their plates. Chase took the empty chair beside Amber.

"This looks delicious," she said, leaning toward him slightly.

27

Their shoulders touched and her soft, barely there scent of springtime wafted over him drawing him closer. "If it's not good you can blame Rafe. He's the one who put them on the pit. I just took them off."

She brushed her hair out of her face and his gaze locked on her soft lips. "I don't think there will be a complaint."

She straightened, breaking the brief contact and took a bite of the steak. Immediately she shot him a thumbs up. "Perfect," she murmured.

Looking at her Chase couldn't have agreed more—she was perfect in his book—and that was a major problem.

Amber and Sadie headed over to the church the next morning to check on the wedding decorations. When she saw the church she understood immediately why it appealed to Sadie with its postcard perfect white wooden exterior, the tall white steeple and stained glass windows.

It was simple, inviting and perfect for a small intimate wedding.

Sadie paused outside the door. "Norma Sue, Esther Mae and Adela are here decorating. You'll love them."

"Is that the posse?"

Sadie's expression turned mischievous. "It is. They love everything about weddings and I'm crazy about them, so when they offered to help decorate I couldn't say no."

Amber knew about the three older ladies from articles that had been written in the Houston Tribune for several years by a local reporter about Mule Hollow, the small town that advertised for women to come and marry their cowboys. These three ladies had been the ones who'd sent out the invitation that had saved the town one wedding at a time, as women had begun to show up, fall in love and marry their cowboys. It was a great story but Amber wasn't interested in being one of those women. She had not come here looking for a man but to get away from one.

Sadie paused on the steps. "You, my single friend, need to watch your back. I think I saw a bullseye on it."

"Ha. Only if I say so. I'm only here for a month—at the most—and then I'm heading out," she emphasized as they walked inside.

"I'm still holding out for more."

Amber chuckled—she might find Chase

Hartley extremely attractive but even that hadn't swayed her to start dreaming about country life. "You are dreaming."

"I certainly can."

"You made it!" a red headed woman in her sixties called from the front of the sanctuary when they walked into the front door. Dressed in bright yellow sweat suit with sparkling stars all over it, she rushed off the podium and fast walked their way, elbows pumping as she came.

"Amber, this is Esther May Wilcox."

The redhead surveyed Amber with bright green eyes full of speculation. "Nice to meet you."

"You too," Amber replied, wary of that look. Feeling she might need to turn around and hit the road especially as the other two ladies in the room gathered around.

"Norma Sue Jenkins and Adela Ledbetter Green," Sadie introduced.

Ranch woman Norma Sue Jenkins, a robust woman with kinky gray hair, stuffed her hands to her wide hips and grinned. "Glad you've made it."

"We certainly are. Sadie needs her best friend on this special weekend." Adela, the third woman was dainty, with a cap of stylish white hair framing a face dominated by huge blue eyes, kind eyes…wise eyes. "I'm glad to be here with her," Amber said. "Y'all are doing a beautiful job."

"So, you're single too," Esther May cooed, all of Amber's warning bells now ringing when she looked at the redhead.

"Happily so," Amber told her firmly, which only made her chuckle and wave her hand as if swatting the notion aside like she'd swat at a fly.

"You are going to love it here," Esther May continued at a fast clip. "We've married off our fair share of eligible cowboys but we have so many we've only seemed to make a dent in the situation."

"That's right," Norma Sue agreed, grinning from beneath the white Stetson that sat on her head of wiry, gray curls. "Look at your friends here, they've gotten two good ones in those twins. Why, those boys are hardworking, successful and know how to treat a lady. And…they look good in the saddle—being a ranch woman I tend to think that is a requirement." She hooted with laughter.

Amber laughed too as she met the robust woman's twinkling eyes. She had to agree with the sentiment after seeing Chase riding that horse the day before. The man and the image he made riding that gorgeous horse just would not get out of her head.

"Okay, so tonight we have the rehearsal dinner and tomorrow is the wedding," Sadie said. "I'm still in shock that I almost made the mistake of my life just a month ago."

Amber agreed with that. "I'm glad you found out about the man before you married him. The rat-fink. He's just lucky I wasn't with you when you found him and his secretary all hugged up."

The posse' frowned.

Esther Mae placed a hand on Sadie's arm. "I'm so glad you found the "rat-fink" out before you married him." She grinned at Amber. "I *like* you. You've got gumption. Isn't that right girls?"

Adela nodded. "Gumption and cowboy'n go well together."

"Like Roy and Dale Evans," Norma Sue quipped.

And suddenly Amber's back itched. That bullseye felt heavy between her shoulder blades.

CHAPTER FOUR

That evening at the rehearsal Amber's back was still itching from the idea that the posse might have their sights on her as a target for some of their meddling. She'd witnessed the excited twinkle that lit their eyes earlier that afternoon. Clearly they were invigorated by the idea of marrying off young couples.

But as she took Chase's arm and practiced walking down the aisle to the back of the church following Sadie and Rafe she had to fight the attraction fluttering in the pit of her stomach. She was all too aware of him and that the posse was watching from the back of the church, speculation and excitement lit their expressions. She had more on her plate than worrying about being the target of their newest wedded bliss campaign but she had the feeling that was exactly what she'd become. Not that it would do them any good because her life was back in Houston.

"You two look plum cute together too," Norma Sue said to Chase and Amber as they reached them. "Now, Norma Sue, a beautiful woman makes any couple cute," Chase drawled.

Amber pulled her arm from the crook of his. "I may not be so cute tomorrow when I'm wearing heels and wobbling down the aisle. I don't play well with heels all the time." It was completely off subject but she had no intention of joining into a conversation that revolved around her and Chase as a couple. She glanced at Ty and Dalton who were standing a few feet away where they had been watching the ceremony. They would act as the ushers—really handsome ushers.

They were gorgeous cowboys but looking at them did not cause her pulse to flutter nor was her gaze drawn to them every other moment that they were in the room as she was finding was true of Chase. And why were Norma Sue, Esther Mae, and Adela not looking at them as possible matches for her if they were starting to zero in on her as their new target?

"I need to check my messages before we go in for the rehearsal dinner." It was true but also an excuse for a time-out. Picking up her purse from the table at the back of the church she headed out onto the front steps. Space. She needed it.

And she really did need to check her messages to see if there had been any news about whether they'd been able to apprehend the man who'd been following her.

Her phone rang as she stepped onto the front lawn of the church and without checking the caller ID, she slipped it from the front pocket of her purse and answered it.

"You messed up. Messed up more than you realize," the menacing male voice growled.

Amber gasped and her fingers tightened on the phone. She didn't have to ask who this was. She knew. "Leave me alone," she snapped.

"You think leaving town is going to stop me from finding you? Think again. I'll find you and you'll pay for taking what was mine."

"I just told her what she needed to hear—"

"You'll be sorry you ever meddled in my life," he threatened and then the line went dead.

Amber's heart raced and she felt breathless as a knot of anger and fear lodged together in her chest.

"Amber, are you all right?"

Startled, she swung around, her heart

fluctuating erratically. Chase stood on the grass only a few steps away. How much of the conversation had he heard—not that it was a long conversation.

"I'm…fine." Her words were unsteady as she fought to regain her composure.

He looked skeptical. "Well, pardon me if I contradict you but you sounded alarmed and in trouble and you're white as a sheet right now." He stepped closer. "Not to mention looking like you're going to pass out any minute."

She stared at him. "Well, I am fine. And I assure you I have no plans to faint." The last thing she needed was Sadie finding out about this. She inhaled sharply and willed her pulse and her heart to regain its footing.

She didn't want Chase telling Sadie what had happened.

Dusk was settling in and there were shadows everywhere as she looked around. She shook off the knowledge that Ned Talbert might be looking for her. There was no way he could find out where she was. She needed to inform the detective about this though.

"Look it was nothing. I need to get back in there." She started around Chase, intent on halting this conversation because she suddenly had the unexplainable urge to tell him everything that was going on. Every worry she was having.

"Amber you and I both know that conversation *wasn't* nothing. It's your business though."

She moved to go around him again and he gently grabbed her arm and stopped her.

"But I'm here if you need me for anything," he said then dropped his hand.

"I'm fine," she reiterated once more and forced her feet to march her back to the reception hall and the dinner that was underway. But the warmth of his hand on her arm and the thought of having his strong shoulders to lean on was overwhelmingly tempting.

It was a little after nine and Chase had gone straight to his office after the rehearsal dinner. He had some last minute paperwork to do preparing for the big pre-Thanksgiving bull and cattle sale they were having during Rafe's honeymoon time. He welcomed the work, needing something to occupy his mind other than thoughts of Amber.

He couldn't shake the feeling that Amber was in some kind of trouble.

"You still working?" Ty asked about an hour later. Leaning a shoulder against the office door, he stared across the room where Chase studied the computer screen.

"I'm nearly through. Then I'll be able to take up some of the slack while Rafe runs off on his honeymoon."

Ty grinned. "You could always tell him he can't leave."

"Yeah right." Chase laughed, rubbing his eyes. "How's that colt doing?"

"It has great promise. A colt like him doesn't come along that often so I'm enjoying working him."

Ty loved his horses and ran the horse operation for the ranch. CC had hired him on a few years earlier and Ty had been building a solid horse division for the ranch ever since. And he was as dependable as any man Chase had ever met. Voices came from the hall and then Rafe and Dalton entered his office. Suddenly the large room that had once been CC's office seemed small with all the partners except Maddie stuffed into it.

"Hey," Rafe said. "I wanted to take a moment to thank y'all for letting me go off and get married right now. I know with the cattle sale coming up next week that this isn't the best time for one of us to be away."

Chase put on his poker face. "We'll expect you to do double time when you get back,"

"Whatever it takes I'll do." Rafe grinned. "But I figure I'll fill in for each of you as you tie the knot."

Ty got a wary look on his face. "On that note, I'm calling it a night."

"Hey, I'll go with you," Dalton said heading after Ty, At the door he halted and with a half teasing, half serious glance at Rafe he fired back. "I'm glad for you Rafe but I am in no hurry to settle down. May not ever."

"Boy, you do know how to clear a room," Chase told Rafe as Dalton followed Ty out, their boots could be heard clomping up the stairs seconds later.

Rafe shrugged. "You're still here.""I was here first. You aren't about to start thinking that just because you're happy everyone has to get married are you?""No," Rafe scoffed. "But when a man is happy he naturally wants his friends to be in the same arena."

"I'm doing just fine in the arena I'm in thank you very much."

Rafe settled into the leather chair across the desk from him. "Fine. I'm not pushing. That's your business. I came to ask you something else."

Chase pushed back from the desk and leaned back, relaxing in the cushioned chair that had belonged to CC. "Shoot, whatever you need I'll do. You know that.""Yeah, I do. But after what was just said you might not like this one very much. Sadie caught me a little while ago and said she was worried about something going on with Amber. She has a job that has her dealing with abusive individuals sometimes, and sometimes it's not safe. Sadie is worried about a case she's working right now."

The phone call. Chase sat up in his chair. "What's going on?"

"She encouraged a woman to take her child and go into a safe house for abused women. That's what she does. She's used to dealing with these situations but this time it really must have hacked off the abusive boyfriend because he found out who she is and was following her before she came here. She's been advised to take some time off while they try and locate this guy. Sadie is afraid she could be in a little danger, that maybe the man is stalking her."

Chase leaned forward, every muscle tensing. "Did he follow her here?"

"She's not sure."

"Has she called the police?"

"Yes. They are working the case and they're the ones who advised her to lay low for a while. The wedding was at the perfect time and she's planning on staying a few weeks. But Sadie is worried that something could happen while we are gone. She's convinced Amber isn't telling her everything. It's not my place to disclose this to everyone because Amber's keeping it all to herself. But we know you'll be discreet and wanted to ask you if you'd look out for her while we're gone? It will help Sadie not worry if she knows you've got Amber's back."

"I'll watch out for her. I've figured out she's pretty hard-headed. Got a mind of her own."

Rafe grinned. "Well, to hear Sadie talk, Amber can take care of herself. Sadie just has an uneasy feeling. Thanks, buddy. I'll keep you up to date on anything more we learn."

Later, Chase found himself not sleeping as his mind kept turning to Amber. The woman worked at a hotline center for abused women…that surprised him.

But being stalked—just how dangerous was this job of hers?

CHAPTER FIVE

Saturday arrived with a slight chill in the air. November had arrived with all of its unpredictability that always accompanied it. Thanksgiving Day was only three weeks away and having lived in Texas all her life Amber understood that November was a swing month—it swung up and it swung down on the thermometer.

Today was the wedding day and all the guys had headed into town early for breakfast at Sam's Diner—a very nostalgic place that she was anxious to see herself one day while she was here. It had been mentioned a lot in the articles Molly Popp-Jacobs wrote for the paper. But not today, today was about Sadie.

Tugging her light sweater closer around her Amber walked across the ranch yard to the barn and the arenas. She hadn't looked at the ranch yet and was curious about it. Plus, she didn't want to take a chance that Sadie would overhear her talking to the detective and Amber needed to fill him in on what Ned Talbert was up to. The man had called two more times during the night but recognizing the number she hadn't answered her phone.

The barn was actually a horse stable and she was greeted by several friendly horses as she walked down the center of the stalls toward the back exit where double doors were opened wide to an outer fenced area. Though she'd seen ranch hands milling around various areas of the other barns this area looked secluded enough. Her shoulders were tight as she dialed the number.

The detective answered on the second ring. "Crawford here. Miss. Rivers," he barked gruffly even before she could identify herself. Amber assumed the he had looked at his phone's ID prior to answering his direct line. "How are you faring out there? Anything to report?"

She quickly relayed what had happened and Crawford took the information in without saying much. When she was finished he asked a few precise questions for clarification.

"At this moment we have no info to suggest he knows how to locate you there at your friend's home. We've dusted your apartment and found no prints. He's covered his tracks but like you, we're pretty certain Ned Talbert was inside your apartment. Did you have anything written down, say on a piece of paper on your desk that might leave a paper trail to you there?"

She thought about that hard. "No. I know Sadie's number by heart and there were no invitations sent out because the wedding is on such short notice, so he wouldn't have seen anything to tell him where I am. I'm assuming he got my phone number off the Internet?"

"Most likely that's correct. Again, we're looking for him and think we have a lead. Keep me posted and I'll do the same."

Not knowing what else to ask him she said goodbye and disconnected. She felt more discontent now than she had prior to the call. Her shoulders hurt they were so tight with tension.

"Are you alright?"

She jumped and spun around at the sound of Chase's deep voice. He was standing a few steps behind her. His Stetson shaded his eyes but she could still see and feel the intensity of his gaze as they bore into hers.

"I, I'm fine." The strain in her voice was

evident and she saw in his expression that he heard it too.

"Why are you so skittish?"

"I'm not—"

"Yes you are. Even Sadie has noticed it. She asked Rafe to ask me to look out for you while they are gone."

"No she didn't?" she gasped. But it sounded just like something Sadie would do. Amber would have done it for Sadie. Despite not wanting to worry Sadie she had because she'd figured out that Amber was downplaying the situation. Her friend knew her too well.

"That woman is too perceptive. I didn't want to worry her while I was here. And I don't need you to look out for me."

"Well, she is worrying and I don't want Sadie worrying about you while she's on her honeymoon so I'm going to do as she asked. Rafe told me that your job could be stressful and dangerous sometimes."

Frustration clawed at Amber—how much had Sadie revealed to this cowboy? "I work at a crisis call center. I work with abused women. We get them help and get them out of a bad situation and into hiding if need be."

"Is that what you've done? Helped a woman hide?"

She nodded, not sure how much she wanted to share with him.

"Did you make an abusive husband angry? And don't look so shocked. I figure that's where the danger has to come from if the boyfriend or husband finds out who helped their woman disappear."

She nodded, giving in she sighed. "I helped a woman on Monday. It had been the third time she'd called in and something told me that this time she really needed out and she might not call back. I assured her that she and her little girl would be safe if she just trusted me. And she did... Sadly, in a moment of weakness she later called him after she was in hiding and told him what she'd done—"

"She *called* the guy?"

"It happens all the time. I don't understand it, but it is not uncommon. Thankfully she regretted it immediately and knew she couldn't take her child back into that situation and they were able to relocate her once more but—"

"But that didn't help you. She told him where she'd gotten help and who had helped her."

Amber nodded. "Yes, we just didn't realize

she'd exposed that info until he showed up in the shrubs at my condo and then followed me later and threatened me."

"So, he is stalking you?" His brows crunched and his jaw tensed as anger flashed like quicksilver in his gorgeous eyes.

"A little."

"Stalking is stalking once or twenty times. Especially if he's got a reason to hate or hurt you."

There was something in his voice that set her on alert. "You sound like you know what you're talking about."

He shook his head. "Just concerned for you. What are the police doing?"

She didn't believe him. The way he'd grown white beneath his tan told her something wasn't right.

"I have a restraining order on him. They weren't able to match his prints inside my apartment but feel certain the break-in was him. I made sure I wasn't being followed here. They will find him by the time I get home and everything will be fine."

"And what if they don't?"

"I can't live my life afraid. I can take care of myself. I teach other women how to defend themselves I can do what I teach."

"You wouldn't stand a chance against this guy if he really wanted to get at you."

"That's pretty presumptuous of you." She pinned him with a direct challenge.

He held up his hands. "Whatever you say. But I'm just going to tell you that Sadie is asking me to watch you and I don't want her worrying while she's on her honeymoon. I've promised her and promise you, that nothing is going to happen to you on my watch."

The idea of being watched over by Chase had its appeal.

The truth was—it was *too* appealing.

That appeal was even stronger when Chase had walked into the church with Rafe and Cliff the hour before the wedding started. Amber's mouth had gone dry seeing him dressed in the pristine white shirt and western cut tux. All through the wedding her attention kept straying to him instead of being riveted to the happiness of Sadie and Rafe exchanging vows.

Each time their gazes locked her heart tumbled and her stomach dipped…it was the most intense feeling Amber had ever experienced. It didn't make sense.

And yet it was there between them. Undeniable.

"I now pronounce you husband and wife. Rafe you may kiss your bride."

Amber was startled by the words of Pastor Chance Turner.

Over. Already.

Amber focused. It had been a beautiful wedding and exactly what Sadie deserved. Amber just had been too distracted by the best man. Now, she riveted her attention to the happiness on Sadie's face as Rafe gazed down at her sweet friend. Peace for her friend filled her. Looking at Rafe's expression of love as he leaned in and kissed his wife for the first time. Tears sprang to Amber's eyes. This was the look of love her friend deserved.

All women deserved that look, deserved the kind of man who would cherish her in sickness and in health. Who would take care of her and protect her…Amber worked with so many women who didn't realize they deserved this.

Amber sighed softly as Rafe continued the kiss and hoots and good wishes were shouted out. Rafe kissed Sadie like he never wanted to let her go.

Wiping a tear from the corner of her eye she

caught Chase watching her. He smiled and her heart fluttered in response.

Tearing her gaze away she returned her focus back to Rafe and Sadie—it was safer there. She had enough to worry about right now without adding being attracted to the self-assured cowboy. Especially now that he was determined to keep her safe.

There was something about his self-assurance when it came to protecting her that got to her despite the fact that it would be useless to even think about acting on the attraction.

Wouldn't it?

CHAPTER SIX

The reception was held at the Mule Hollow Convention Center. It was a renovated space on Main Street that had been converted to hold events. Not a convention center by city standards but for a tiny town like Mule Hollow it was perfect.

Amber's mother had arrived a few minutes before the wedding from the bed and breakfast she was staying at a few miles from town. She was spending the night but leaving early the next morning because she had a large event to cater that afternoon.

Sadie's mother on the other hand, had had a limo deliver her at the church just in time to have a mother of the bride photo snapped of her with Sadie and Rafe. The limo was now waiting down the street for Susan Archer and would deliver her home sometime late tonight. Amber had been afraid Sadie's mother might not even stay for the reception but she'd surprised them and announced that she'd be there.

Looking like a million dollars she sat at a table with Amber's mother. Amber decided she'd have to give her mother a surprise thank you gift because she was helping distract the high strung society mom from the quaint surroundings. Burlap table runners and twinkling white lights strung from the rafters was nothing compared to the ice sculptures and silk she'd had planned for the wedding fiasco Sadie was supposed to have had a month earlier with the ex-slug of a man…okay, Amber reeled in her disgust of the ex. She had to stop holding a grudge and just be thankful that Sadie had discovered his lying and cheating ways before she'd married him.

There was always something to be thankful for.

To be honest, Amber should find the slug and give him a huge hug for letting his true colors shine in time for Sadie to run for the hills and fall in love with Rafe.

Amber was glad that this wedding was nothing like the extravaganza it would have been if Susan had been allowed to "help".

"One more happy couple," Esther Mae squealed excitedly over the band tuning up in the background. She came hustling over from the punch bowl. "It was a lovely wedding. Where's Chase? Y'alls dance will be coming up soon. And I know you're looking forward to that. I saw you lingering over him during the ceremony."

Lingering. Amber choked on a cookie. Esther Mae slapped her on the back.

"There there, don't get so excited."

Amber's teared up from wheezing as she wondered if anyone else had noticed that her gaze kept straying to Chase during the ceremony. Thankfully Chase had been busy since the service and she'd lost track of him while she'd been visiting with her mom and Sadie's mother. Now she let her gaze roam the crowded room as the band began to play *From This Moment* and Rafe led Sadie out onto the dance floor, took her into his arms and they began to move slowly around the room.

Amber had forgotten she was supposed to dance with Chase. Her throat went dry thinking about him holding her in his arms.

"Isn't that romantic," Esther May sighed. "I never grow tired of happy beginnings."

"Its happy endings, Esther May," Norma Sue said moving from the punch bowl to where they were standing.

"I know what I said. I like the beginnings too."

Amber smiled at that. She liked the beginnings too.

"Hey there, partner," Chase said, coming up from behind her. His warm breath feathered across the back of her neck. "We're up next."

Amber's skin warmed and a shiver rippled across her skin as she turned her head to see him. Big mistake since it put her very near his lips. She swallowed hard and forced her gaze up to meet his. He was watching her with a smile in his eyes. "Don't look so excited about the idea, I promise I won't step on your toes."

She smiled. "Thanks. But I'll warn you I'm not very good at dancing."

"And I don't believe that for a minute but no worries. I'll lead."

Her heart fluttered in her chest and anticipation filled her.

When the band called for the wedding party— which consisted of her and Chase, he slipped his hand around hers and led her out onto the dance floor. Sadie and Rafe smiled from where they still stood swaying in wait of them to join them on the dance floor. Amber was startled by how nervous she felt as Chase took her into his arms.

She placed her hands on his shoulders and butterflies tumbled and fluttered through her. She was more nervous than if she were standing on the edge of a skyscraper—and for a girl terrified of heights that was pretty nervous.

"Relax, I've got you," he said and took the first step.

She stepped on his foot. "I'm sorry!"

He chuckled. "I wore my protective footwear so it's all good."

She laughed and immediately did it again.

He grinned. "Breathe," he whispered softly and she felt some of the tension ease from her.

"Okay, let's try that again," he said.

She held his gaze and when she felt him take a step she went with him—not on him.

"You're doing good," he said after a few steps.

"I haven't ever been much of a dancer so it must be that you're a good leader." Oh he was that alright. The man moved smoothly around the room in perfect time to the music.

"Why don't you relax and let all the tension I feel in your back and shoulders ease up for a while?" He shifted her closer into his embrace and she found his smooth jaw against her temple.

And there was no way she could relax then. Her pulse skyrocketed and her knees even felt weak as everything about Chase Hartley filled her thoughts.

Engulfed her and Amber felt as if somehow she was floating.

Chase was fighting hard not to pull Amber close. He'd known her for a total of barely two days and the attraction and protectiveness he felt for the strong-willed woman was nearly overwhelming. She smelled of soft soap, a simple fresh scent that drew him and tilted his senses off their axis. He'd been thinking about her situation ever since being told about the man stalking her. He planned on keeping her in his sights at all times while she was here but he knew she wasn't going to be receptive to feeling smothered. That left him with a dilemma. How to keep her close without trouble.

"Do you ride horses?" he asked as he led them in an easy circle in time to the music. He'd never been a huge fan of dancing but at the moment he was grateful for every moment he'd ever spent on the dance floor. It was now enabling him to hold Amber in his arms. He reminded himself that she was not his type. She loved city life and had no plans for small town life, so even a mild flirtation was dangerous in the event that there could be a possibility of more between them. He was playing with fire.

"I ride," she admitted lifting her face to his. A smile teased her lips and teased him. "But it's a volatile proposition."

He laughed. "Well if I promised to give you a few pointers—or not—totally your call on that. Would you like to take a ride in the morning?"

She studied him. "I would love that. I'm actually wondering what I'm going to do while I'm here. I'm not used to sitting around."

"You'll figure something out. Main thing is that you're safe."

She stiffened immediately and he berated himself for reminding her that she was in danger. The music ended and she stepped out of his arms. He wanted to pull her back and keep the dance going. "So will you go?"

"Yes, I might as well get the whole experience while I'm here."

He smiled. Tomorrow was going to be a good day.

By the time Sadie and Rafe had been covered in birdseed and driven away in Rafe's truck, traditional cans and ribbons rattling behind them down Main Street, it was late. Amber offered to stay and help clean up but everyone waved her off and told her to go spend a little time with her mother. Sadie's mother had left right after the newlyweds left so Amber followed her mother out to the Victorian B&B where they sat on the front steps and visited for an hour.

"So tell me about Chase, the good looking cowboy you danced with tonight."

Amber should have known her mother had been watching. Unlike Sadie and her mother who had always had a strained and somewhat distant relationship Amber and her mother were close. They'd overcome a lot through the years after her father had left them.

"He's one of the partners of the ranch that Sadie's husband is part owner of too. He's a nice man. But, Mom, he's a cowboy and he lives and breathes ranching."

"And you don't?"

"Funny, Mom. You know I don't. It doesn't matter anyway, I'm only here for a few weeks and then I'm back to my work." She'd told her mother about Ned Talbert but she'd told her as little as possible. Mostly that she had an angry boyfriend on her hands and disappearing for a while was the best thing to do. She did not tell her that he'd been stalking her and that he'd started calling her. There were just some things a mother didn't need to worry about.

"You work too hard and worry too much about other people. Promise me while you're taking this break you'll consider the possibility of change in your life. I'm not saying this Chase is the man for you but I could tell he was very interested. And he held you so gentle and respectfully." She smiled. "That's what a mother wants for her child."

Her mother had never had that. Like so many women who'd been abused by their husband Amber's mom had lived a lie for years before Amber's dad finally left them. "Every night I try to help women realize they deserve a good and decent man in their life."

Her mother took her face in her hands and looked at her deeply. "And so do you. Just because your father left us when you were small does not mean you don't deserve a good man. I just don't want you to forget that."

Amber stiffened. She hardly ever let herself think of her father. "I know that, Mom. Me still being single has nothing to do with him. I just haven't found the right man in my life."

Her mother's expression softened. "I know. But just try to enjoy your time here in this darling small town among these sweet people."

Amber leaned forward and kissed her mom's cheek. "You got it, supermom," she said, calling her mom the nickname Amber had given her many years ago. "Now I guess I'd better hit the hay. I'm going on a horseback ride tomorrow."

Her mother clapped her hands to her cheeks. "With Chase?"

"The one and only."

A smile of satisfaction lit up her mother's face. "That sounds like the start of a perfect adventure."

Amber was still thinking about the adventure quote a little while later after she'd said goodbye and was at the ranch. As she crawled into bed she couldn't let it go. This could be an adventure...she deserved an adventure. It wasn't as if she truly believed Ned Talbert was going to get at her and hurt her. Ned didn't scare her, not really. But he was giving her a break from her ordinary life and well, it wasn't every day that you found yourself stuck in a small town with a hunky cowboy offering to be your protector.

She crossed her arms and stared up at the ceiling where the reflection from an outside lamp had the lacy outline of tree limbs outlined. She smiled.

Yes, whenever she was given the okay to go back home she would but right now she was going to relax and let herself enjoy a little adventure.

Cowboy style.

CHAPTER SEVEN

When Amber walked into the kitchen the next morning Ty and Dalton were leaning against the counter drinking coffee while Chase was flipping pancakes. One look at her wearing boots with her jeans tucked into them and Chase completely forgot about pancakes. "You already look like a country girl. You brought jeans and boots with you?"

She laughed. "Not hardly. I'm a city girl in disguise. I found these in Sadie's closet. Thankfully my foot isn't too much smaller than hers but my legs are far shorter therefore the pants had to be tucked in or rolled up and they really looked funny rolled up."

"All you need now is a horse," Dalton drawled, reminding Chase his partners were there too.

"And a hat," Ty said, indicating with a nod the wall rack where their hats hung on pegs.

Chase strode across to the rack and lifted one. "This one is Sadie's."

Amber crossed over to him, took the hat and plopped it onto her head.

"What do you think?" she asked with a sassy smile.

He studied her. "Perfect."

She blushed and he realized he might have been looking at her like she was the last cinnamon roll on the bakery shelf.

He smiled. "For a city girl, I mean."

"Great. Today I'm getting my country on. So, where's my horse?"

"Sit down and have a pancake or two and then I'll introduce you to your ride."

He started back toward the stove and found Ty and Dalton both struggling to hide their laughter. He could only imagine what they were thinking because he knew they'd realized that for a moment there he had forgotten all about them being in the room.

"You boys wanna grab some plates?" he drawled giving them both a warning look, daring them to say anything.

Chuckling under their breaths they both dove into action, one grabbing plates the other silverware. Chase knew that for now they were going along with keeping their teasing to themselves but later…he'd better get ready because it was coming.

Amber loved the beautiful horse that Chase saddled for her. The mare was a sweet tempered chestnut that stood completely still as Amber slipped her foot into the stirrup and hauled herself into the saddle. Being short made the learning curve of mounting a horse a little more tricky than if she'd had long legs.

"I could have helped you," Chase offered as she finally sank into the saddle and managed to get her feet into the stirrups.

"Nope, thanks but I did it. Though I'm thinkin' a pony might be more my speed."

"You'll get the hang of it after a while," he said and then took the time to give her a few pointers on riding. "Now have her walk a little bit and then tug on the left rein and have her circle back to me. You can do it."

Amber did as he'd told her and gave Delta a little nudge with her knee more than clicking her heals against the horse like Amber had assumed was the way she should do it. But he'd told her that Delta reacted easily to nudges and it didn't take more than a slight one to have her doing what her rider wanted. And he was right, just a few slight movements and the horse reacted with amazing obedience. "She's so responsive."

"Yes, she is. That's Ty's doing. We all know how to tame a horse but Ty is the official ranch trainer and has a special touch with the animals. You're seeing a product of his talented training. He takes pride in his job and is making a name for himself."

"Well I feel very safe on Delta."

He placed a hand on Delta's shoulder next to Amber's knee and looked up at her. "I just wanted to make sure you know how to give her some basic demands. You never know when something will spook a horse and if you know how to control her then the situation is not a problem. But if you don't then it could be a wreck."

"A wreck?"

He smiled. "Yeah, it means when the horse and the rider get into a bad situation—they have a wreck. Same as with a car it's just a different mode of operation."

"I see. Well I'll try very hard not to have a

66

wreck."

"I'd appreciate that. We want you in one piece at the end of this visit." He strode to his horse and Amber felt a bit jealous of his long legs when he swung easily into the saddle of his golden horse. Watching him, a lump lodged in her throat—goodness he made a horse look good.

He led the way out of the yard and into the pasture behind the barn. Amber rode like she was sitting on a jackhammer and was beginning to think she was going to bounce straight out of the saddle.

"This isn't as easy as it looks," she admitted, her words chattering with the jarring ride she was making. She had to hang onto the saddle horn and there was no doubt that tomorrow, if this kept up, she would be one sore woman.

"Sit back in the saddle," Chase urged then explained a few adjustments to the way she was riding.

She shifted and was grateful when she found herself in smooth motion with Delta. "Amazing. Of course I could have lost a few pounds by the end of the day if I'd have been able to handle the reoccurring impact."

"Then again you might have lost a tooth or

two."

She laughed then. "Most likely that would have been the case. Thanks. This is actually better than I thought."

"Well that's encouraging since we haven't even gotten out of sight of the barn. There's hope for you yet, city girl."

She tugged on the brim of Sadie's hat to straighten it since it had bounced to a crooked angle on her forehead. "I decided last night to look at my time here as an adventure. So that's what this is. I'll be heading back to the city soon enough but while I'm here I might as well enjoy it rather than gripe about it."

He looked thoughtful. "That's a good way to look at it. I've always said living on a ranch is an adventure. When I first came here I knew ranching was where I wanted my future to be. I can't imagine ever going back to the city."

Amber jerked her gaze to him. "You're a city guy?"

"Hey, don't look so shocked. I spent time during college at my roommate's ranch and I was hooked. My parents own a company that makes computer parts. The idea of being inside a building all day like my dad did not appeal to me so I made my own choice. I—"

She leaned forward and rubbed Delta's neck and Chase paused for a minute watching her. She turned her head and studied him. "What were you about to say?"

He laughed. "To be honest, I got distracted and completely forgot."

Amber's stomach felt suddenly bottomless and her pulse accelerated. "Flirting will get you nowhere, Mr. Hartley."

His dazzling eyes held hers and her pulse kicked into high gear.

As if reading her mind his tempting smile widened. "You sure are sure of yourself. What happened to the adventure part?"

"That kind of adventure is not what I'm looking for—" but she was suddenly thinking about how his kiss would feel. "Um…learning to ride a horse without breaking any bones is a good start. But I doubt I'm up for riding a bull or anything but maybe I can go watch y'all work the cattle or something. Sadie said it was actually fun."

His forehead crinkled. "I'm not sure getting hot and sweaty would be classified as fun but we'll sure get you out there."

Amber's stomach tilted and the air seemed very

humid. "Oh, fun," she said then nudged Delta and got to moving. This conversation had become way too distracting.

Yes she'd decided to look at this as an adventure but falling for this handsome cowboy was not part of the adventure. And Amber had a feeling that if she wasn't careful that might happen. Which was something she'd never thought would happen.

"You ride good for a beginner," Chase told Amber after they'd ridden in silence for several minutes.

"Thanks. I'm actually enjoying it. It's kind of inspiring."

"Well I think so. But how do you mean?"

She colored a little. "I sometimes try to write children's books. And well, I was just thinking about a story I started a long time ago. I can't tell you how long it's been since I thought of that story."

This was a surprising twist to her personality. They had been riding beside the stream and he decided this was a good place to let the horses take a drink. "So write it," he said, halting Nugget and dismounting. He strode over to her. "Let's let the horses take a break. And I want to hear about the abuse hotline gal who wants to write children's stories."

"That sounds good. This is a gorgeous place." She started to dismount and he placed his hands around her waist and lifted her to the ground. After all the trouble she'd had maneuvering herself into the saddle he didn't want her falling while trying to dismount for the first time.

"Oh," she said when he surprised her by the move. She placed her hands on his shoulders and looked a little embarrassed as he placed her on the ground. Only problem then was he didn't want to let go of her.

"I think horseback riding agrees with you," he said softly. Fighting every cell in his body crying out to kiss her. Just like a school room full of unruly children he struggled to get control. His heart was throwing a ruckus as he dropped his hands to his side and took a step back. Amber was watching him and probably wondering what in the tar he was doing.

It couldn't be helped though it was getting harder and harder to move away from her whenever he made the mistake of getting too close.

"There's a pretty spot up there with some

shade." He turned and pulled a couple of bottles of water from his saddle bag and handed one to Amber. Her fingers touched his and sent shards of warmth exploding through him and instant thoughts of kisses and romantic sunsets.

Her breath caught softly as if she felt it too. Without saying anything she unscrewed the top and took a couple of quick gulps. Then she turned and marched toward the area he'd indicated.

He followed her and tried to talk some sense into himself. This woman he'd just met would be leaving here when the police department gave her the green light. He wasn't leaving and so this overwhelming attraction didn't make sense. No sense at all.

And yet he was having no luck talking sense into himself by the time they reached the rocks that were large enough to sit on and listen to the gurgling stream.

"So tell me how you got into crisis work? And where this forgotten dream of writing children's book fits into the pages of your life."

"Bullies. I hate bullies and was always heading in this direction from the first day I saw a boy picking on a girl at school. I smacked him in the nose with my fist and it begun from there."

"You smacked a guy in the nose?" He laughed. "I'm getting a mental picture of you doing that."

"I did it alright and spent the afternoon in detention. It was worth it. That girl went on to date guys in school who treated her badly and it killed me."

"You have a kind heart."

She shrugged. "I do but I just want to make people aware. To stop as many children as possible to not have to go through a hard life of abuse and abandonment."

His instincts went on alert. "Is there something about that scenario that applies to you?" He thought of her mother and the successful, strong business woman she appeared to be.

Amber studied him. "No one has ever asked me that question."

He saw a vulnerable look pass over her before she pushed her shoulders back and inhaled deeply as if resetting her emotions.

"My mom was abused by my dad. Strangely enough she loved him and begged him to get help so he could be in our lives. In my life. She's always maintained that he was a good man but that he'd come home from the war tormented. Of course I loved him, and didn't understand the times he hurt

73

Mom. But rather than get help or continue to harm us, he abandoned us. So there lies my infatuation with helping women in need. My mother nearly died from what my dad did to her before he left." She ran a finger along a ridge in the rock edge. Then lifted her gaze to his. "I'm a mixed up cookie."

He couldn't help himself as he gently laid his hand over hers. "You're an amazing woman, cookie whatever you choose to call yourself. You're truly something good. And now you have someone's angry boyfriend threatening you and stalking you. Do you ever think about getting out of that line of work? Maybe write that book."

"Why would I, I love what I do. And I know that I've saved lives through my work. Besides, I shelved the idea of the book years ago. I don't have time to write it and it's hard to sell to the children's market. Besides, I've never found an idea that seems good enough."

He squeezed her hand and pulled his away not wanting her to have to pull hers away or make her feel uncomfortable. But he'd rather have pulled her into his arms and taken the pain away that he'd glimpsed in her eyes. "For your own safety is one reason you might consider giving it up."

"I'm careful and contrary to what you may have heard, I don't get stalked every week. This is an unusual case."

"But it's happened before?"

"Yes. Look, I came out here to ride today. Not talk about this. Okay." She stood up and he did to.

"I'm just concerned for you, Amber."

"I'm used to looking out for myself, Chase. And I can take care of myself. I also know self-defense."

He lifted his hand to run a thumb along her cheek. "Maybe it's time you let someone else in."

"Maybe," she managed. "But that's not as easy as it sounds. Not for me. I've been defending myself since I was a kid."

"But you're not a kid dealing with kids anymore. This is a man."

"I'm stronger and well trained. You can't talk me into being scared. I refuse to be."

His brows met as he tensed. "Now that's just—" he bit back what he'd wanted to say. There was absolutely no reason for him to alienate her because he didn't agree with her line of thinking. It took everything he had not to finish saying her idea was ridiculous. That wasn't exactly the way to get her to cooperate with him. "You're a stubborn woman but you're also smart. So please don't do anything…ah, stupid."

She cocked her head to the side and hiked a brow. "I'm not planning to."

He was overcome by the need to protect her. And he had to remind himself that maybe he didn't need to do anything stupid.

But as tensed up as he was feeling that might be harder to do than one would expect.

So the adventure had taken a detour during the horse ride. Chase had caressed her cheek and she'd thought he was going to kiss her.

And she'd wanted him to.

But she wasn't giving into that temptation and his overprotectiveness had helped her keep her head on straight. Yes there was a part of her that longed to have someone to rely on but then there was that side of her that couldn't let her guard down long enough to do that. If she let her guard down she could be hurt. That knowledge was enough to keep her firmly on her side of the boundary line.

They'd silently backed off from their stance and had ridden horses for another couple of hours and she'd really enjoyed it. The ranch was pretty and to her surprise she liked riding.

As they rode into the yard she could see Ty working with a young horse inside the arena. Chase saw her watching him and they paused and sat on their horses for a few minutes watching.

"That's a colt he's getting ready to train to be a cutting horse."

Ty looked at ease and in command as he held a rope tied to the colt's halter and let the colt trot in a circle around him. After a few minutes she followed Chase to the barn and they dismounted.

"You want to brush Delta down? I can do it if you're ready to go in."

"I'd love to. Just show me what to do."

He removed the saddle and then handed her a brush from a bucket next to the stalls.

"Just long smooth motions," he said, demonstrating his technique. Amber watched his shoulders bunch with each movement and the gentleness he used as he took care of the horse. This was a man who might be overprotective but he would never harm a woman. He was a good man. She forced herself to focus on the horse and not his movements. She copied what he was doing as she ran the brush over Delta.

But despite their disagreement that morning, she had enjoyed every moment she'd spent with Chase.

But that did not mean she was going to be stuck in Mule Hollow for up to a month and have an escort everywhere she went…and that was going to have to be made clear pretty soon.

But right now, she was enjoying the view far too much.

"You're doing good. Delta is enjoying it."

Her knees wobbled when he smiled at her. She reminded herself that she was not wanting or needing to be attracted to him. To a cowboy. It would only complicate things and wasn't her life already complicated enough?

The afternoon sun filtered through the windows of the barn and seemed to suddenly shift so that he was illuminated in the sunbeam. The air in the stables just evaporated. Poof, Amber was completely breathless.

She had never been more attracted to a man in her entire life…

CHAPTER EIGHT

Chase had been fighting frustrations all morning. He'd started out thinking about kissing Amber and now he was about to bust with the need to hold her. And she was looking at him as if she felt the same way...which was confusing because he knew that being attracted to him was not on her bucket list.

But at the moment she was the only thing on his bucket list...or on any list.

Heaven help him the look in her eyes broke him. He stepped forward and before he could talk himself into some good sense, he'd slipped his hand around the nape of her neck, then lowered his lips to hers. He wasn't thinking...

Wasn't analyzing.

Wasn't anything...just kissing Amber.

That was all that mattered.

The plan—well there was no plan—but his

intent had been to just brush a quick kiss across her lips. A quick kiss to satisfy the internal force driving him…but she sighed…

And he lost it.

He'd moved his lips across hers feeling the response as she'd moved to meet him with her own kiss. Instantly his hands had moved to tangle in the thick strands of her hair and he felt as if Amber had been all that he'd ever been waiting for. All that he'd ever wanted. He deepened the kiss wanting to be as close to her as he could get.

She was small and he had to dip slightly to hold her closer, she reacted by placing her arms around his neck and instantly she fit against him like she'd been made for him.

Her heart pounded against his and for a moment time for Chase was lost.

Delta's soft nicker broke the moment and Chase pulled away, as the world kept spinning and Dalton strode into the barn.

"Oh, hey…" he stopped short and grinned as he looked from Chase to Amber. "Sorry to bust in on y'all. I was just going to say that it's my turn to cook tonight and I wanted to see if burgers on the grill worked for y'all?" He chuckled. "It's a mighty nice evening out. Supposed to be a full moon I think."

Chase wanted to whip himself for embarrassing Amber like this. He scowled at Dalton then glanced at Amber, she looked a little dazed—no more than he felt.

She shot him a glare. "Dalton fix whatever you feel like. I'm perfectly fine with anything."

And then she walked out of the barn without a glance in Chase's direction.

"So, you and Amber. I was wondering." Dalton leaned against a stall.

Chase was not going to discuss Amber with anyone. "I like her," was all he was going to say.

"No law against that. She's a beautiful woman. And you're about due a little time in the relationship department."

He went back to brushing Nugget down. "If you're just going to stand over there butting into my business then pick up a brush and finish grooming Delta."

Dalton picked up the brush and took over where Amber had left off. "I noticed how you were looking at her at the wedding. I suspected this was going to happen. And of course I noticed the posse birds eying you too. So I figure you better get prepared. This is going to get interesting—

especially once they figure out there's a possibility."

"Dalton, I just kissed her okay, and the posse isn't going to know that unless you go telling them. So, I'm warning you not to embarrass Amber any more than she already is."

Dalton scowled. "My friend, you are delusional if you think those ladies aren't going to know. I suggest you start wearing sunshades when you and Amber are within any visual distance of each other because even then, those ladies will know. Heck, I figured at the wedding it was only a matter of time."

Chase finished brushing Nugget and let the horse out into the pen next to the barn and tried to get hold of his temper. When he turned back to Dalton he pinned his partner with a glare. "It was a kiss. Just a kiss."

Dalton grinned as he dropped the brush in the bin. "You keep telling yourself that. But I've never seen this side of you before. It's plum entertaining."

He strode past Chase and headed out of the barn chuckling all the way.

Friends. Sometimes it didn't pay to have them.

Truth was Dalton had his number and he knew

it.

There was no way on earth that that kiss would ever be classified as "just a kiss".

That kiss…had rocked his world.

After the kiss of a lifetime. Forever more known to Amber as "the kiss" she'd managed to make it through the evening with Chase and his partners…she'd been so grateful when Maddie and Cliff had shown up to join them. They were all preparing for a big bull and cattle sale happening the next day.

Having another female in the group to have a conversation with had helped ease some of Amber's tension as she'd focused most of her attention on talking to Maddie. Oddly, Chase seemed to not be bothered in the least about the kiss or the fact that Dalton had caught them smooching in the barn like teenagers.

Maybe it was the fact that he and the others were discussing the busy day ahead and he was intent and focused on all that would go on. But if his actions were any indication at all it was as though nothing had happened on the horse ride or in that barn.

Not that it mattered…okay it mattered. It mattered a lot because as much as she hated this had happened with a cowboy who lived in the country the undeniable fact was that Amber had never, ever felt a toe curling, heart pounding kiss like that before.

It had felt like…more.

Like her very heart would ache forever if he stopped.

How could that be?

Just thinking about it made her skin tingle and her gaze swept the area in search of Chase. She'd known him for such a short time and yet it was as if that kiss had connected with her heart…and that was the stunning part—Amber didn't open her heart easily.

It could not happen again and that she knew for certain. They as a couple didn't make sense. Him here having chosen this life and her there in the city she loved.

No sense at all.

"Earth to Amber," Maddie said, drawing Amber's thoughts back from the land of "the kiss".

"Oh, sorry. What were you saying?" Amber asked realizing she'd been lost in her own thoughts.

"I said, it's going to be a busy day. There will be buyers from all over arriving with the intent of buying our commercial heifers and bidding on the bulls we've raised."

Amber focused on the needs of the ranch and not her own situation. "What can I do to help?"

Maddie thought for a moment. "If you want to help with registration in the morning that would be great. And though I'll be helping with penning and sorting after registration Chase will be running the books and the lineup…in short he'll be ramrodding the thing. So maybe you could be his assistant."

Amber groaned silently. Of course he would need an assistant. And of course that would be her. Just peachy. "What do I need to do," she asked and tried not to let her ill temper seep out.

"You just hang close to him and if he needs something then you get it for him so he can field all the questions that are going to come his way. There is an unbelievable amount of paperwork keeping a sale running smoothly. And though Chase is a master organizer he might need a hand during this. It's our first major sale since CC passed away and the truth is we're all a bit nervous."

The guys were all nodding now and agreed in their manly ways, startling her that they would admit such a thing. Chase had set his burger down and was tapping his fingers on the table as if thinking. He stared down the table to where she and Maddie sat.

"That's a perfect idea, Maddie. Amber, would you be willing to help out like that?"

Amber shrugged. "Sure," she quipped telling herself that at least it sounded like it was going to be a busy day.

Turned out busy was an understatement. Amber was awake and in the kitchen by five a.m. as the entire household was up having breakfast and preparing for the day to come. She'd not slept well as she'd suspected and seeing Chase looking fresh and in control the moment she walked in to the room unsettled her all the more as every cell within her jumped for joy seeing him. The moment he shot her a smile over the brim of his coffee, she couldn't think straight.

He wore starched jeans and a starched western cut shirt in a spotless white that was definitely not meant for working cattle. Today he would be the man behind the running of this sale not the man running the cattle.

It struck her in that moment how really important this day was for all of them at the New Horizon Ranch. They obviously had prepared for today prior to Sadie and Rafe's wedding and had it planned out in a manner so they were able to relax in the few days during the wedding proceedings. But now, it was all about getting it done. And like Maddie had said the night before they wanted to make CC proud.

Amber realized she wanted to do everything she could to help them. Even spend time with Chase despite her personal need to stay as far away from him as possible.

Now, he was standing beside the coffee pot. Directly in the line of Amber's morning sanity.

"You fellas look ready to tackle everything this day will bring," she forced out through tight jaws. Ty and Dalton greeted her, though her attention was riveted to Chase. She was determined not to act as if she were thinking about that kiss—though she was. She absolutely was as she marched past him toward the coffee pot. Dear goodness the man smelled like morning kisses—not good she reprimanded as he shot her a sexy smile that had her all but stumbling into his arms. He reached for the carafe and she picked up one of the mugs from the mug tree and prayed her hand didn't shake as he poured the dark brew into her cup.

"Mornin'," he drawled, studying her as he poured. "Thank you for helping us out."

"I'm glad to," she said, taking her coffee and moving a few steps away from him so that she was out of the danger zone—of both his scent and the magnetic force around him that had her senses flipping out like a trapeze artist.

She didn't know much in that moment but she knew this...it was going to be a very, very long day.

CHAPTER NINE

Trucks with trailers came in droves and Dalton and one of the ranch hands directed them where to park. One of the pastures beside the barn had been cleared of cattle and the gate opened so there was room for the slew of vehicles that were pulling in by seven that morning.

Amber sat at a table next to the barn where a registration sign, placed on the barn wall behind, them told buyers where to come. She and Maddie were busy and so were the guys. Chase had his computer notebook rather than a clipboard and she could only imagine the spreadsheets and facts he was using to run the sale program. They'd hired an outfit to handle much of it but he was still a very busy man.

The barn that sat directly across the wide rock parking area between the house and the barns and arenas was where the sale was being conducted.

She hadn't been in there until that morning. It was set up for sales like this with a show pen inside where the heifers and bulls would be while the auctioning was being conducted. Buyers bid from the bleachers that were set up across from the pen.

She was surprised when local folks from Mule Hollow started showing up. The posse ladies were some of the first to arrive.

Adela's husband Sam was working at his diner and couldn't get away so she'd come with Esther Mae and her husband Hank, a balding cowboy with a twinkle in his eyes. Norma Sue and her husband Roy Don came too. He was foreman at Clint and Lacy Matlock's ranch and they arrived early also. Theirs was a huge outfit down the road from New Horizon and Lacy also owned the Heavenly Inspirations Salon in town. She was a primary cohort of the matchmakin' posse. At the wedding Amber had met Lacy and many others, including Sheri, her co-owner of the salon. She'd also heard of them all through the newspaper articles so she had already begun to feel like she was meeting old friends each time a new connection was made. She wondered if they would be at the sale today.

Maddie nudged her elbow. "We'll go sometime

this week to have coffee with Lacy and the gang at the diner. Lacy and Sheri both had a baby last month and had baby checkups this morning so aren't coming to the sale," she informed Amber as if she had read her mind.

"I'd love that," Amber said.

"It's always a good time when the girls all get together and it'll put you in the know about everything."

Amber chuckled at the way Maddie drawled the words and arched a brow. "You're going to love this group more and more as you really get to know them better. I promise."

It sounded great to Amber since it meant an excuse not to be hanging around Chase, something she was realizing was only going to get harder to do with every moment that passed. It was like he was a potato chip and she wanted more.

Amber had had a long conversation with the Lord last night since it was a little disconcerting that she would suddenly be so infatuated with a cowboy when a cowboy was so wrong for the plans she had for her life.

After the men got registered they all went to inspect the cattle and decide what they planned to bid on.

The posse stayed beside the registration table.

"It's nice to see you settled in and looking right at home here," Esther Mae said, looking bright in her teal pants and bold pink blouse spouting a huge butterfly…it reminded Amber of the butterflies that were holed up in her chest ready to take flight each time Chase came near.

"I'm helping out," she said. "And learning all about ranch life."

Norma Sue stuffed her hands on her hips and glanced toward the group of men gathered around Chase and his other partners. "That handsome Chase showing you around? Y'all sure seemed to hit it off at the wedding."

"He took her riding yesterday," Maddie offered and under the table she bumped Amber's knee. Amber bumped her right back and caught the twitch of her lips as she obviously fought off a smile. Amber bumped her knee again—not finding the fact that the matchmakin' posse was eyeing her with keen interest in the least bit funny.

"Riding!" Esther Mae said. "Oh that's always a fun thing. Maddie, you sure are glowing this morning. I see Cliff over there helping out."

Maddie smiled. "Esther Mae you glow pretty good yourself."

The redhead winked. "Well, I do love my Hank. After all these years that man sets me to glowing…sparks are flying all the time."

Norma Sue harrumphed. "Too much information, Esther Mae."

"Don't be looking at me like that, Norma Sue. You know you're just as crazy about your Roy Don."

"Ladies, let's not get carried away," Adela interjected drawing her friend's attention then smiling at Amber. "Sorry they get excitable sometimes. So you went riding. Did you enjoy it? This is beautiful country."

Amber could just feel the wheels turning in their minds as they all three smiled expectantly at her. "Um, yes. I did," she said carefully certain that she didn't want to share too much information. "I haven't ridden much in my life and I enjoyed it. We rode to a stream and it was so peaceful." There, that was enough information but not too much.

"Oh it sounds romantic," Esther Mae cooed.

Amber almost groaned. Thankfully a new group of people walked up to register and she got busy while the ladies moved to the side and began talking among themselves.

"Don't let them bother you," Maddie said quietly as she and Amber waited for the cowboys they were helping to fill out their registration forms.

"They're really focusing on me and Chase aren't they?"

Maddie looked at her with a comical expression of disbelief. "I don't think you realize that you watch him when he's in a room. You may not want to be interested but you are and it's apparent to everyone. But he does the same thing with you."

The cowboy asked Maddie a question on the form and she shifted to answer him. Amber took the moment to let what Maddie said sink in. Did she really watch Chase so much that it was noticeable? As if in answer she suddenly realized that involuntarily her gaze had shifted and she was watching him speaking with a group. He was so handsome—his gaze shifted and suddenly connected with hers. It was just briefly, but they connected as if they were alone beside the stream once more. Then he shot her a quick smile before focusing back on the conversation he was engaged in.

Amber had to pull her gaze away and only then did she feel eyes on her. Glancing guiltily toward the matchmakers she found all three of them watching her. She smiled weakly and then went back to work. She had the feeling she was in trouble in more ways than just with the posse. She was in trouble with the feelings she was starting to have…and after only a couple of days around Chase.

What was she going to do after an entire month had passed?

"So what makes a good heifer?" Amber asked Chase a few hours after the sale had started and she was now acting as his assistant.

Chase had been wound pretty tight all morning. Between handling the sale and any problems that might arise he was also dealing with Amber's nearness. And thoughts of wanting a repeat of the kiss the day before.

She was distracting on so many levels that he feared he would make mistakes on the paperwork if he wasn't careful. He propped his elbows on the bars of the pen and studied the pair in the stall that she was staring at. "Basically a commercial heifer is bred to be a good mother and to be able to carry her babies well. So we look for good feet. He pointed to the heifer's side and the area there in front of the back legs, she needs to be deep there, like from the backbone to the underbelly there needs to be depth because that's where the babies will be carried and we like to give them room. So along with a few other things we're looking for that's what you want to look for. And uniformity. You want cattle that all have a similar look so your herd has a consistent look."

"And here I thought a cow was a cow."

He grinned and relaxed a bit. "Nope. Now you know—probably more than you wanted to know."

"And I have a feeling you skimped on what you could have told me."

"I didn't want to see your eyes glaze completely over. By the way, thanks for doing this."

Their shoulders were nearly touching and he had to fight the urge to stand closer to her and inhale—the soft scent of her. He held his ground though.

"You're welcome. It's giving me something to do and like I said, it's an adventure."

"It is that." A rough one for him as he had to force himself to focus. "One I better get back to. Looks like the auctioneer is ready to start. Come sit with me."

"I'll be there in a minute, if that's alright. I need to make a few phone calls first."

"Sure. I'll be over there near the auctioneer for easy access. Is everything alright?" He yanked his mind off of his own wants and searched her expression. She didn't look tensed up or anything but he berated himself for not having thought more about everything going on in her life right now.

"I just need to check in. I'll see you in a few minutes."

He watched her walk across the yard to the empty arena where Ty trained his horses. She was safe, he told himself. There was no one to bother her and he couldn't smother her or she would resent it. Making himself move, he went to do his job.

But his mind remained on Amber.

Amber moved away feeling his gaze following her. She was checking in but also she needed some space. Moving through the crowd into the sunlight, she made her way to an area near the training arena where no one was around and then she called her co-worker Jill.

"He calls every day, Amber," Jill informed her immediately. "He asks for you and wants to know when you're coming back. He won't say who he is and despite that his number shows up as unknown on the ID, we all know it's him. It's creepy, Amber."

Amber's temper spiked. She knew the information should have scared her but it made her mad. Who was this man to disrupt her life like this? "Don't worry, Jill. They're going to catch him soon. I have a feeling he's going to do something very stupid. I'm safe so no worries. Okay? Promise me you won't stress over this. You have that baby you're carrying to worry about not me."

Jill was seven months pregnant and had had a lot of trouble making it to this stage in the pregnancy. She didn't need added worry and since she was a natural nurturer she worried a lot. "Promise me."

"I'll try but you stay low. I know you don't worry like I do but, Amber, this is serious. This guy creeps me out."

Amber's anger intensified, pushing any fear into the background. Right now she was more concerned for Jill than for herself. "I'm fine. You should see these cowboys I'm holed up here with.

They'd rival any of those cowboys in those romances you're always reading about." Jill loved to read and always had a paperback or an ebook beside her desk for the downtimes between calls. Jill chuckled and Amber instantly felt better.

"If I wasn't happily married and expecting this beautiful sweet girl of mine I might be jealous. Instead, I'll just be very happy for you and hope you take this time off to enjoy the scenery and maybe fall for a cowboy. That would be so romantic—"

"Whoa. Stop right there. You know where I'm at, right." Amber knew that Jill knew where she was because they'd talked about Sadie's wedding. But she was one of the few people who knew. She also knew that this town had a reputation as the town that had advertised for wives to marry their cowboys.

"Yes, I know exactly where you are. The town where love is in the air and the hair...that's the thing that Lacy Brown was quoted as saying when Molly first started writing about that town. So go to her salon and get your hair done and see if you find some of that love floating around in the air. You're due some of the good stuff."

"What is it with everyone caught up in this

matchmaking?" Amber was not about to let anyone know that she was actually feeling off-centered because of the overwhelming sense of attraction she kept feeling toward Chase. It was too fast, too not right, too far from her work. Meaning it would never work so why was she even letting herself be tempted by it?

Because "the kiss" had been too good.

"So have you met Lacy and the matchmakers? Have they found you?" Jill cooed.

Oh no, this was all she needed. "No. I mean, yes I've met Lacy briefly, she's very nice."

"I knew she would be. What about the matchmakers? Come on spill."

"Yes, I've met them too. And they are just like the articles portray them...very intent on keeping this town thriving by marrying folks off as quick as they see a spark of attraction between anyone—"

"So they've spotted you crushing on someone? I am so excited!"

Amber groaned. She hadn't meant to let that slip. "Look if you saw these single cowboys you'd understand. It's nothing. My work is in Houston, remember?"

"There are other jobs. And even if you wanted this job you know there are ways to hook the hotline up so you could work from home. I had that option remember?"

Amber knew it was true. The owner of the privately owned abuse center had offered to do this for Jill when she was home with her baby girl but she'd opted to leave the hotline after the baby was born. With the way Jill worried about all the callers it was probably the best. She needed to focus herself on being a mother and not on worrying about so many others.

"I know that, but I love the city and I'm not sure I'd like feeling disconnected from the office. I'm feeling a bit like I'm swimming out here alone right now." "

"Well you're not. The police are working the case and you've got me here. You call more and let me know how you're doing with the posse and the cowboys. I'm hooked now that you've let on that you're in their sights."

Amber chuckled. "Don't get your hopes up is all I can say. Okay I'll talk later. You take care of that little girl."

After they finished their goodbyes and hung up Amber stared out across the pastures and let her thoughts roll over everything she'd learned. Ned Talbert was a loose cannon it seemed. The man was reckless though and she just wasn't going to let him worry her. He was being reckless. They would catch him.

She only had to stay low and wait.

But, it was the staying low here with the matchmakers breathing down her neck and Chase getting under her skin that worried her.

If the good Lord wanted to totally shake up her world then he'd achieved success because she was royally shaken. And it had nothing to do with Ned Talbert stalking her.

CHAPTER TEN

"At thar is sure a good un," Applegate Thornton, the hard of hearing retired rancher, boomed from behind Chase and Amber.

Chase had introduced Amber to App and his buddy Stanley Orr as soon as the two men had sat down behind them on the bleachers. They loved cattle auctions and had been busy pointing out the pros and cons of each animal. Thankfully they were impressed with the New Horizon stock and there was more pro than con.

"Yup," Stanley agreed and spat a sunflower seed to the ground. "Yor right about that. If I was building up a new herd I'd buy that one."

"Ole CC would have been proud," App added slapping Chase on the shoulder.

"Thanks, App. You too, Stanley. That means a lot." The bidding ended a few minutes later on the final heifer and Chase felt a sense of relief. This had been the first sale since they'd inherited the ranch and he hadn't realized how tense he was. He'd learned a lot from his mentor and former boss who'd been his benefactor. Chase took what he'd been willed seriously and planned to build on the legacy that CC had left and dreamed of.

Stanley scratched his balding head and gave him and Amber a speculative study. "Norma Sue and her meddling crew are right—you two make a mighty fine match."

Chase cringed and caught the startled look in Amber's eyes. If the woman only knew how her eyes gave her away she'd wear shades all the time. He didn't blame her it was like the town had a one track mind suddenly. He'd never been in the matchmakers sights before and so he'd never experienced this interest until now. He clearly understood why some of his friends had gotten upset when they were wearing targets on their backs. Rafe and Cliff he didn't think had ever had it this strong though. They'd managed to fly under the radar a bit...not a luxury he was having at the moment. And Amber was not happy about this at all and he could tell by the stiffening of her body. But she smiled. It was forced but there.

"We're not a couple," she informed the older

man.

"You should be, you look like you get along good. Don't they, Stanley?"

"Like two peas in a pod. While that thar auction was going on y'all was jest a workin' together on that computer like y'all were of one spirit. It was a nice thing to see."

Chase had enjoyed having Amber beside him helping him with his work. And she'd relaxed, though after she'd come back from her phone call earlier she'd seemed a little tense for a while. He needed to ask her about that.

"I enjoyed helping out." Amber's gaze shifted and Chase figured she was searching for an escape route.

App boomed again, "You two coming out to Cort and Lucy's place on Friday night? They're having that shindig to raise money for the shelter."

"An early Thanksgiving bash for all the families who the shelter has helped," Stanley interjected just as loud. "They're raising funds for the future moms and kids who come there."

App hiked a brow. "And they could use all the support they deserve."

"That sounds like something I'd like." Amber's expression brightened and she gave App her full attention. "Anything to support a shelter and I'm all in."

"We'll be there," Chase assured them.

"You don't have to take me," Amber said, causing both older men to frown.

"Well why wouldn't he take you?" App boomed, his lean face drooping into a fold of wrinkles. "He's a smart young fella and yor a pretty young woman, he's probably chomping at the bit ta escort you out thar."

Stanley chuckled. "You can see it in his eyes."

Great. He really didn't need their help. Chase saw what looked like exasperation flash on Amber's face. "Okay, fellas," he said, taking control. "We'll take it from here. I'll bring Amber and we'll see y'all there. Thanks for coming out."

Amber's eyes narrowed at his agreement, no doubt she'd been trapped by Esther Mae and her buddies this morning about him. He'd suspected as much when he'd seen them hovering around her at the registration table. The matchmakers had picked up on the energy that passed between him and Amber when they were around each other. And whether Amber liked it or not it was there.

And it was undeniable.

Amber watched the last of the vehicles and trailers pulling out of the yard that afternoon and she breathed a sigh of relief. She had never felt so much pressure from well-meaning folks in all her life. It was like they all had a one track mind. She'd finally sought out Maddie when she wasn't busy and just asked her what their problem was and Maddie had assured her that they weren't always so pushy. But when they thought they had a match in sight they got a little zealous.

Zealous, ha!

And Chase hadn't helped the situation at all.

She was sitting on the patio drinking a cold glass of tea when he came striding across the gravel parking area toward the house. She swallowed the lump that lodged in her throat watching his long strides and fought hard to focus. She was mad at him.

"Hey," he said in greeting giving her a crooked grin.

She set her tea down. "Hi."

"Look, I know you're not happy about what happened earlier. You left pretty quickly after App and Stanley did."

"I'm not happy. Chase, I can take myself to this

benefit. You just tell me where it is and I'll drive myself. I don't know if you noticed but everyone in this town now has us as a couple. That's not good."

He sat down at the table across from her. "It's harmless. I guess I should feel bad that you've shot me down that quick though."

She colored slightly. "Look, this—whatever it is between us is a bad idea. That's just the way it is. My life is in Houston. So I'm being practical. And focused. I'm here only temporarily."

"I get that, but I also know life has a way of getting in the way of the best laid plans. I'm speaking hypothetically here, so you're telling me your life is so well laid out that you have no room in it for change? No matter what?"

Amber didn't like that question…

Chase realized instantly the question bothered Amber. She took a deep breath and looked away from him, out to the pasture. He studied her profile and realized he could look at her all day. Forever. She was a complicated woman and figuring her out could possibly be a great adventure. Okay, so he was getting a little carried away.

"I'm just saying," she said looking back at him. "That if I do decide to change my life that it will be my plan."

"So no room in there for God's plan?" So he was playing hard ball now. But no one ever got to call the shots on their whole life. "Okay, sorry about that. I didn't mean to sound preachy."

"Thanks because I was going to say that my plans are so solid because I do believe that's God's path in my life."

There was absolutely no comeback to that. "I still want to take you, one, because I want to and two, because I promised to look out for you while you're here."

She stood up and he did the same. "I don't need to be watched every hour of the day. This guy has no idea where I am. He has been calling the center everyday trying to find out when I'm coming back so he certainly doesn't know where to find me. That means you sticking with me all the time is a waste of your time."

"I don't think so. I've enjoyed the time I've been getting to know you. But I get what you're saying. When did you find out about the calls to the abuse center? That call you made this morning?"

She nodded. "My friend, Jill, she's my co-worker said so. He's driving them crazy and she's really worried about me. It infuriates me that he has me jumping through hoops like this and scaring my friends. Jill is pregnant and has been at risk and doesn't need to be worried about me."

"He's dangerous and going to make a mistake. You just have to stay out of his way until he does and he's caught." He realized giving control of her life over to others was not something Amber was good at. He sympathized with her. But right now she had to. But looking at the flame in her eyes suddenly he knew he had his work cut out for him.

Amber stared at Chase and tapped her boot on the flagstone thinking. She wasn't sure she could do this after all, let Ned rule her life even for a little while. She'd had it on her mind all day. "I'm not sure I can just let someone run my life like this," she said, voicing her concern.

"You don't have patience do you?"

He had no idea how his concern for her was affecting her. On one hand she wanted to walk into his arms and hand over her care and protection. Then on the other hand she had always fought her own battles. She'd relied completely on herself and the very idea of trusting her care and protection to someone else, the police or him terrified her. Put that on top of letting Ned interject fear and control into her life and she was really, really having a struggle.

"I have patience on some things. But this isn't just about me right now. He's got my friends worried and is harassing them. And I've never had patience for bullies."

He surprised her with a smile. "I like your attitude." His expression grew serious. "Something tells me though, that it's driven by something in your past."

"When a girl has no male to stand up for her she can either get trampled by the ones who will take advantage of that or she can stand up for herself."

"You stand up for everyone."

Amber ran her boot along the ridge of a piece of flagstone. "I like to hope so."

"You do. Now let me stand up for you at least right now."

"I can't," Amber said and knew it was true. She just couldn't do it.

Late into the night Chase sat at the computer in his office going through data. He'd pulled up everything he could on the Internet about Ned Talbert. There had been a surprising amount of stuff. The man was an avid hunter and loved to have his picture and his trophy in the paper. He also was a business owner which surprised Chase. This man had a lot to lose and yet he was still harassing Amber and the people who worked with her in order to find out information. That bothered Chase.

The guy wasn't worried about himself at this point and that made him a dangerous man.

CHAPTER ELEVEN

The morning after the sale Amber tugged open her door and walked out into the huge house. She peeked down the short hall from her room toward the kitchen, pausing to look around the corner into the living room with the long staircase up to the second floor. No one was in sight.

Relieved, she headed into the empty kitchen and grabbed a piece of paper from a pad beside the phone. She assumed everyone was either out and about on the ranch working or in the barn. She knew though that Chase was somewhere near and she needed to hurry if she were going to avoid him. She scribbled a note telling him that she'd gone to town and would be back later and left it on the counter by the coffee pot. Then she hurried outside to her car.

Ty was the only one she saw and he was out in the arena working with his colt.

Sliding behind the wheel she started her car and backed up then headed toward the exit.

Once she made it to the paved road she breathed a sigh of relief. She felt like a kid sneaking out, but the more she'd thought about it during the night the more she knew she couldn't continue to have Chase following her around. For one, she was safe and she completely believed that. Two, the man had begun to be on her mind all the time. His kindness and interest in her last night had played with her emotions and it was just simply too dangerous being around him. Too tempting. Her life was in the city.

There was only so much that she could do on a ranch. She had enjoyed the ride but if she fell for a cowboy she would not spend all her days on a horse. She would not spend all her days twiddling her thumbs sitting at the ranch waiting on him to come home every evening from his work. She would go crazy. And, yes there was the option to have the hotline directly routed to her anywhere, but she had a life outside the abuse center and it was a full life. She loved her self-defense classes that she taught. She enjoyed being involved. What was there for her to do that would even come close to fulfilling her passions? Become a matchmaker like everyone else it seemed? Ha!

She was still looking at this as an adventure but an adventure required getting out and about and that was exactly what she was doing. The fact that she hadn't just come out and told Chase this disturbed her. She had a feeling the stubborn man wouldn't have listened anyway so...here she was driving into town like a runaway teen. It was silly.

She saw the town before she reached it. It sat in the distance from the four way stop like a colorful ghost town in an old western sitting on the horizon. Stark outlines against a blue cloudless sky. And in the center the bright pink second story of a building rose up like a beacon.

Amber pressed the gas and sped toward town sighing happily when she reached it. The cute, colorful town was adorable.

Who wouldn't want to live here?

Her. It was great for a day trip though.

She parked in front of the dress shop that was a couple of doors down from the pink building which she knew was the hair salon, Heavenly Inspirations. Curiosity filled her as she got out of the car and scanned the town. Quickly, she stepped onto the wooden sidewalk and moved to the dress shop window where a beautiful dress was on display. Then, spying the candy store next door she headed that way. Chocolate would make her feel better and she really thought under the circumstances that she deserved a treat.

Pushing open the door a cowbell clanked and three women behind the counter greeted her with smiles and hellos.

"It smells heavenly in here," she said smiling back at them. She immediately noticed that one was very timid, standing back slightly and letting the other two take the lead.

One of them stepped forward. "H, hi we're glad you're here. Um, can we help you?" she asked then glanced at the lady beside her who gave her an encouraging smile.

Amber studied the assortment of sweets. "I'm in the mood for chocolate."

"We have plenty of it," the encouraging smile lady said. Amber figured she was in charge, maybe even training the others. "All varieties and it's all handmade with the finest ingredients. We make it in the back and if you see anything you like we can bag it up for you."

"It looks absolutely wonderful." Amber searched the assortment of candy, caramels, chocolate and all manner of sweets. On the end were a lot of pastries and cakes too. And she moved to look at them. They were beautiful though simple.

"We can make you any cake you like," the timid lady said. "We do all occasions and weddings too."

"Did you do my good friend Sadie's wedding cake?"

The young woman in her bare twenties beamed. "Oh we did."

"It was amazing. Both gorgeous and tasteful. And so moist. I adored it."

"Thank you. Thank you very much," the young woman said and glanced at the smiling lady beside her. "Becca taught us. She can do anything."

"From the looks of what I see here I would have to agree." Amber tried to figure out the three women. Becca was the owner or manager maybe. Whatever she was, she was talented.

After Amber figured out what she wanted she paid for it then took her bag. "Thank y'all I can't wait to enjoy this."

Yes, this was what a day trip was all about. Treating herself to specialty candies topped the list. Out on the boardwalk she paused to break off a piece of the pecan caramel fudge and pop it into her mouth. "Oh. My. Goodness," she muttered as it melted in her mouth. She closed her eyes and savored the velvety flavors. Someone knew how to make candy. This was not the average chocolate. She popped the second half of that piece into her mouth not even considering waiting. It was amazing.

"Amber! Woohoo!" Esther Mae called hustling her way across the street.

"Hi, Esther Mae. How are you?"

"I'm better than a snail in a turtle shell," she chuckled.

"Well that's good." Amber grinned, liking Esther Mae's wit.

"You look like you're doing well, I saw you come out of the candy store. It's divine isn't it?"

"It's delicious."

"Dottie Cannon, our sheriff's wife, she is an amazing candy maker and she teaches all the gals at the women's shelter to make it and run a business. They train right here in the store."

"No Place Like Home, right?" Amber asked, impressed. Until App and Stanley mentioned it yesterday she'd forgotten Mule Hollow had a shelter.

"Yes. It's a wonderful place. Dottie's teaching them a trade and also other things like finances and how to work with customers and like I said, how to run a business. It builds self-esteem while also helping them stand on their own two feet. That way they don't have to rely on anyone for support. Especially their worthless husbands. Or boyfriends."

Amber's mother had opened her catering business and made several mistakes as she struggled to find a way to build a life for her and Amber. Something like this would have been a great program for her when she was starting out. "I had heard there was a shelter. But I thought it was just a temporary home. I had no idea they did all this."

"It's great. It's like a holding pad for them until they can stand on their own two feet. It has a great rate of success. We are so proud of it. You should come with me tomorrow. It's our day to go help."

"I'd love too." This explained the odd situation on the inside of the store. She'd found that sometimes abused women were not outgoing and many of them did need the hope a job or career offered them. She really wanted to see how the place worked.

"Dottie is looking for help you know."

"Oh no, I'm a phone gal. I help get the women

to go for help. I'm not really involved with the actual safe houses." Behind her she heard the roar of a truck engine and Esther Mae's eyes widened as huge a silver dollars.

"Oh dear, Chase looks hotter than a red hot poker!"

Dread slammed into Amber and she whirled around to see the gorgeous cowboy hauling out of his truck like hounds were chasing him—okay maybe not chasing him it looked more like he was doing the chasing and that she might be the one in need of running. She widened her feet stance and automatically braced herself. It was a reaction pure and simple. His eyes were firing lightning bolts and his jaw was tensed up like concrete.

"What do you think you're doing?" he growled stomping onto the plank walk like a bull on a rampage.

"What do you think you're doing?" she fired back.

"Lookin' out for you that's what. I'm here to escort you back to the ranch." He was so close and looking down at her. Amber yanked her shoulders back and stuffed her hands on her hips as she glared up into his incredible blazing green eyes.

"I told you last night I didn't think I could keep

letting this guy run my life. I'm not afraid of him and I'm not ready to go to the ranch."

"You're going if I have to throw you over my shoulder and haul you back."

"Ha, in your dreams, buddy."

He stepped toward her.

"Oh, my you two might want to talk this over," Esther Mae gushed. "And who is "he". Why does Amber need to be afraid?"

"There is no talking to this woman. She knows she's not supposed to leave the ranch without me."

"I—" Amber started to retort but Esther Mae beat her to it.

"Why does she have to stay at the ranch? You two are throwing off sparks enough to burn this town up," she said, her eyes sparkling like she'd just spotted gold nuggets or something. Then they dimmed. "But why does she need to be scared?" Worry amped her pitch up a notch.

"Because she's not safe—"

"Why?" Esther Mae gasped.

Amber glared at Chase. "It's nothing, Esther Mae. The man is overreacting."

"He looks concerned but sounds like he needs to be. What's going on?"

She'd show Chase Hartley some trouble. Oh

yes she would. "I am fine. I had a little problem with a mad, abusive boyfriend of one of the women I helped get to a shelter that's all."

Esther Mae's hand came to her throat and alarm tightened her expression. "Oh, Amber. I hadn't thought about your job being dangerous. Did the man try to hurt you?"

"He's following her," the obnoxious cowboy droned and Amber wanted to kick him in the shins.

"You have a *stalker!* Is he here—in town?" Esther Mae asked looking from side to side as if she'd spot the man lurking not too far away.

"No, he's not here and he doesn't know where I am. So I'm safe and Chase is overreacting. Now, would you *pul-ease* leave," she said to Chase.

"No. I told you. You're coming with me."

"Maybe you should do as he says."

Amber glared at the redhead now. "No, I refuse to be afraid especially when I know I have nothing to be afraid of at the moment. So please don't worry and I'd rather everyone not know about this." It only took a glance to know that she was having a false hope thinking that Esther Mae wouldn't spread this around.

"This is ridiculous," she grumbled, and started

down the sidewalk. No one was telling her what to do—

"Wait!" Chase grabbed her arm just above the elbow.

It happened quickly as she reacted to his touch. She spun grabbed his wrist with her free hand and bent forward twisting just right and in less than four seconds she'd brought him over her shoulder. He sailed through the air and landed on his back with a thud and lay there dazed and looking up at her.

Esther Mae's exclamation of shock reverberated as loud as Chase's grunt upon hitting the planks...

CHAPTER TWELVE

Did that really just happen?

The question reverberated through Chase as he stared up at Amber from flat on his back on the rough, wooden sidewalk. She stared down at him a stunned horror.

It had happened faster than being tossed from the saddle by an angry horse.

"What'd you go and do that for?" he growled scrambling to a sitting position and rubbing the back of his head and feeling a lump. He had to shake the cobwebs out.

Amber was as pink as the beauty shop. "Are you alright?"

"I'm fine," he growled again. His pride was bruised as was his backside but he kept his mouth shut about that.

"How did you do that?" Esther Mae gushed.

Amber stood straight. "I am very well trained.

Despite what people believe I can take care of myself." She glared at him. "You shouldn't have grabbed my arm."

He pushed up from the ground and stood. "You shouldn't have overreacted," he snapped.

"And you shouldn't have grabbed me. What were you thinking?"

He scowled and could feel heat rising from under his collar. "Woman, you're flirting with danger and too stubborn to care." She'd also put him on the ground like a pro but that was because he'd been completely caught off guard. "I was trying to protect you, that's what I was thinking. Now stop being bullheaded and come back to the ranch.""I'll come when I'm ready, Chase, and not a minute before." She turned and started walking again but glanced over her shoulder. "Don't touch me."

"Fine. No problem." He crossed his arms and watched her go. Then he stepped off the sidewalk and leaned against her car to wait. She was in Mule Hollow. If anyone bothered her he'd know it within minutes.

"Wow, she sure is something," Esther Mae said. He'd forgotten she was standing there.

"Something else," he muttered and heard

Esther Mae chuckle.

"Well I've got to run. But I think you're doing a great job. I can't believe someone is stalking her and we certainly don't want anything happening to her. She might be able to protect herself and then again it's always good to have someone who's got your back. Like my Hank…he doesn't have the muscles like you do now but he sure used to. Hang in there."

Chase was relieved when Esther Mae decided to head out. No offense but at the moment he wasn't in any mood to hear about Hank Wilcox's attributes.

He was watching Amber sashay angrily down the street and her attributes, no matter how aggravating she was, were a whole lot more interesting to him than Hank's.

By the time Amber reached Heavenly Inspirations, Esther Mae had hustled up beside her and entered the salon right behind her. Lacy looked up from where she was shampooing someone. Sheri her co-owner and nail tech came out of the back of the salon.

"Hey, hey, hey, Amber," Lacy chimed. "It's

good to see you—Whoa—you're redder than Esther Mae's hair. What's happened to you?"

"Girls, listen up," Esther Mae blurted. "Amber has a stalker."

Oh brother! Really? Amber whirled toward the redhead. "Esther Mae—"

"What do you mean?" Sheri asked first and the others echoed her.

"Nothing. Everyone is overreacting. First Sadie, then Chase and now Esther Mae."

"A stalker is nothing to take lightly," Lacy said. "Isn't that right, Molly?"

"She's right," the woman in the shampoo bowl agreed. "I write for Houston Tribune and stalking makes some sad headlines too many times to disallow."

Great a reporter—the reporter who'd put Mule Hollow on the map with those columns about the matchmakers escapades. "I'm not disallowing or ignoring it. I'm just not in danger here. He didn't follow me to Mule Hollow. He has no idea where I am."

"Are you certain?" Sheri asked. "Have you told Sheriff Brady?"

"I'm certain. And no I haven't had a reason to talk to the local sheriff."

"Chase knows," Esther Mae blurted from her

position by the window. "He's one hot cowboy out there waiting on her till she heads back to the ranch."

Anger shot through Amber toasting her ears. "He's still out there?"

"Oh yes," Esther Mae grinned.

"Well I think that's sweet," Lacy said. "You might not think this crazy person followed you but it never hurts to have a hunky cowboy looking out for you. You've got us too. Right, girls."

"Right," Sheri said, stuffing her hands on her hips, her expression calculating. "You give us a description and you'll have the best look-outs around watching for this dude. He won't stand a chance of getting close to you."

"That's right," Esther Mae harrumphed. "I'll have Norma Sue and Adela in on this in a jiffy and that man better watch out is all I've got to say."

Amber's anger eased in view of their kindness. It actually felt wonderful knowing these women were looking out for her. They hardly knew her. All these years she'd been driven to look out for other women's welfare and now suddenly she had her own little posse to surround her and help her. Tears nearly ambushed her.

"Y'all really know how to steal a girl's thunder,"

she said. "I can't be mad now…even if I don't believe he's coming here to stalk me or harm me, knowing y'all want to look out for me is like nothing I've ever felt before."

"Don't forget about that cowboy out there you flipped over your shoulder. He's wanting to look out for you too," Esther Mae added. "Y'all should have seen her toss Chase to the ground."

"You really did that?" Lacy asked.

"It was just a reflex."

"Some reflex." Sheri grinned and so did the other three.

"Give us his description," Molly said. "We're ready to enlist everyone's help in this."

Amber's mind started working as an idea started forming in her mind. "If the cops can't do something with him then maybe we could lure him here and deal with this ourselves." She was only half teasing as she grinned wide and her eyes sparkled with mischief.

"I love that idea!" Lacy exclaimed. "Let's do it."

"Now hold on," she said. "I was just teasing…" But was she really?

Chase had had too much time on his hands to

think while he waited for Amber to decide to go back to the ranch. He had to admit that he admired her spunk despite the fact that she was being entirely pigheaded. A pretty pig head but still the woman needed to realize that just because she thought this guy hadn't followed her didn't mean he hadn't. Just the thought of something happening to Amber twisted him up inside. He'd known her for less than a week but she meant something to him and he knew it. Amber got to him with her bravery and willingness to help others. She had a strength about her and yet he'd seen a vulnerability in her eyes...she needed someone to be there for her. That dug into him and made him want to protect her and stand by her even when she was pushing him away.

Sadie had asked him to look out for Amber, but even if she hadn't asked him he'd be right here doing it anyway. There was something special about Amber and he wouldn't let any harm come to her.

He pulled out his cell phone and dialed Brady's number. The sheriff was a good friend and also had a real problem with men trying to abuse a woman in any form and that included stalking. A stalker was unpredictable and dangerous. They were not just onlookers from afar and Amber needed to understand that.

"Sheriff here."

"Hey, Brady," he said not wasting any time. "I've got a situation," he said and explained what was going on.

"I'm going to need to talk to her?"

"That's what I was thinking. Maybe if she hears it from you she'll think more about running off by herself."

"Maybe, but she sounds like she's not going to let this creep define her. And that's both good and bad."

"Tell me about it."

He'd just put his phone back in his pocket when Amber came out of the hair salon and stalked toward him—or her car since he was leaning against her driver's door.

"Okay, I'm heading back to the ranch. Does that make you happy?"

He moved away from the car, startled that she was doing like he'd asked. It was almost too easy. He grabbed the door handle and pulled it open for her.

"I can be a gentleman," he said when she looked startled by his actions. "I'm not the bad guy here, Amber. I'm trying to look out for you."

She looked flustered but she softened. "I get that, Chase. It's just frustrating that I have to be in this spot."

He felt for her and had the sudden urge to put his arms around her. He had a feeling there was fear driving her to act so strongly against having help. Maybe even some denial. "I'll follow you." He'd tell her about Brady coming out later.

She nodded and climbed into her car and a few minutes later they were heading home. Ty was at the grill when they walked up the path.

"You two are just in time for my special BBQ chicken."

"Thanks, Ty," Amber said. "I'll be out in a few minutes."

Chase watched her disappear into the house. He normally attacked a problem head on and he didn't seem to be handling this one very well.

"What's going on?" Ty asked.

"I'm not sure. I'm trying to understand her but coming up short."

"Well I'd be coming up shorter than you I can tell you that for certain. I can back you up or whatever you need but understanding the female brain is not a gift the Lord saw fit to give me. Now horses I get, but women I only make a mess of things."

Chase knew his friend had been a bit of a loner since he'd joined the ranch about four years ago. He kept to himself and yet he was always the one who could be counted on to help any time of the day or night. That was one reason he was also one of the ranch hands that CC had entrusted this ranch too. Hard work and dedication had been prerequisites for the honor.

"You and me both," Chase grumbled.

CHAPTER THIRTEEN

Brady showed up the next morning when they were all at the breakfast table. Today there was a lot going on at the ranch. Ty and Dalton had a horse auction to get to and Chase had planned on going too, but instead he was sticking close to the ranch and Amber despite her not wanting him around.

"Has Ned Talbert had any contact with you since you've been here at the ranch?"

"Once," Amber admitted. "He tried calling a few other times but I didn't answer."

"What did he say?"

"That he was going to make me pay for what I'd done.""That's a threat."

She nodded. "But I hadn't reported it to you yet because I'd hoped…well I guess I was just thinking he would go away until I got this last call. I've been worrying since I got it, but with the wedding and being here I haven't taken this step. And I should have." She told him about her apartment and that they were already looking for him and then she told him about how he kept calling the hotline center trying to get information.

"He's not giving up. I'm glad we know now. I'll contact the detective in charge and find out if there's any new developments. Are you going to press charges when they pick him up?"

So this was it. The man hadn't had his girlfriend press charges and he'd been lucky for that. Now it was in her hands… and she didn't hesitate. "I'll press charges," she said, determination hardening her tone.

Chase nodded at her, his gaze serious. "Good. Brady, what are the odds he comes after her here?"

"Pretty high if he finds out where she is. I'd advise you stay low until this is over."

"I've already been advised to stay out of the way until they pick him up so I'll be here." Her stomach felt a little queasy. The stubborn part of her wanted to say no way. That she was going back and refused to be scared. But the saner part of her knew there was no sense pushing buttons that didn't need to be pushed.

"Good. I'll stay in touch. I just want to tell you

that I appreciate all you do for these ladies. They need people to champion them and your willingness to put yourself at risk is heartening. Dottie will want to meet you and I'm sure the ladies will want to meet you too."

"I'm planning to go over there and check it out."

"Great. There's about three families right now who've been with us for several months. One of the women is about ready to go out on her own and she's doing great but the other two ladies are struggling some. They've been through some pretty terrible stuff and it'll just take a while for them to feel confident enough to be out on their own."

"I am so thankful for safe homes like No Place Like Home. It's really a blessing to the women and their children to have a place to turn to in a nearly hopeless situation."

The sheriff nodded. He was a tall, broad shouldered man, reminded her of Matt Dillon from *Gunsmoke*. He looked to be at least six foot three or maybe four and he looked like he could take on the world or a few abusive husbands at a time if need be. Chase stood beside him and was just a little shorter at about six foot one but he looked just as capable of protecting a woman. The thought of his arms wrapped snuggly around her flashed into her mind and she realized she'd been giving him a really hard time over trying to protect her. The man barely knew her and yet he was determined to keep her safe from this jerk who was bothering her. She would talk to him about that after the sheriff left.

A few minutes later with the assurance that he would let her know what he found out or if any new factors came about the sheriff tipped his Stetson at her and left. She immediately turned to Chase.

"I believe I owe you an apology."

"For what?" he asked.

She had to smile. "For being a bit of a jerk about you following me around. You were only doing what you promised Sadie you would do. I'm sorry you've had to do that."

His gaze turned serious. "I might have started out doing it for Sadie but I'd be wanting you safe no matter what," his gaze narrowed then he added quickly. "You or any other woman shouldn't have to be worried about this guy."

His sincerity got her. Of course he hadn't said he was doing it because he cared what happened to her *specifically*. She barely knew him so why was she thinking something like that? Still, something twisted behind her ribs as a lump lodged there. The ache was nearly more than she could take. She didn't need someone looking out for her.

She did the looking out for others.

She'd learned a long time ago not to count on someone looking out for her. It was dangerous. And that was one kind of danger she didn't do any more. That was too risky.

And yet looking at him…she wished… "You're a nice guy, Chase Hartley."

He gave a slight hike of his lip. "You think?"

She laughed at the cute expression on his rugged face. "I think." She didn't tell him that she didn't want him to be nice. She wanted him to be hard to get along with so that her attraction to him could simply be short lived attraction to his looks only. That there would be nothing about his personality to back up the attraction she felt toward him and therefor she would be able to easily walk away from him.

But no. Darn it.

He was a really good guy it seemed and that meant trouble for her.

CHAPTER FOURTEEN

S he'd apologized to him.

Chase mulled that over as he drove toward the women's shelter not long after Brady had left the ranch. Amber had wanted to go and so here they were pulling up at No Place Like Home.

"It's huge," Amber said staring at the rambling two story ranch house with steep roof lines and many windows.

"Yeah, it is. Brady's parents built it in the hopes of having a large family and filling it with children but could only have Brady. He later built his own, more reasonably sized home, married Dottie and together they turned this into the women's shelter."

She smiled. "And finally filled it with children."

"Exactly. Mule Hollow residents embraced it whole heartedly and with the vision Dottie has for it and the way she teaches the women to be self-sufficient it's been a real winner all around."

"Most important it sounds like it gives them the confidence and skills to make it without the jerks they've thought they needed to get by," she said.

He liked her grit. "You're a dynamo aren't you?"

She shot him a bright-eyed glare. "I can't stand bullies. In any form."

"I'm starting to get that. Come on, let's go in." He led the way, but in no way was this conversation ended. Was this personal? Had someone hurt Amber? The idea did not set well with him.

They were walking up the steps when the front door slammed open and a young boy came barreling outside. He slammed into Amber, knocking her backwards into Chase's arms. He caught her as she caught the kid.

"Whoa there, kiddo," Chase cautioned. "You okay, Amber?" he asked, the soft scent of her hair tickling his nose.

"I'm fine." She bent down holding the boy's shoulders. "Are you okay?"

The boy looked to be about eight or so. He nodded. "I didn't mean to run into you, lady."

"Oh, I'm sure you didn't but you might look

before blasting out of that door next time. You're quite strong you know."

He studied her. "I ain't strong. I'm puny."

"And who tells you that? You're young but you don't look puny to me."

He stared at the ground then up to Chase. The kid looked angry and Chase felt for him.

"I weren't no help to my mom when her boyfriend knocked her on the floor. He socked me across the room like I was a pup."

Chase bit back a few choice words noticing the pale yellow bruise now that was fading from the kids jaw.

Amber's expression was full of compassion. "Well I'm glad you're here now. You and your mother are safe. I'm Amber, what's your name?"

"I ain't 'sposed to tell strangers my name."

Smart kid. Chase grinned as Amber smiled at the boy.

"You're right. So, maybe after you get to know me you'll tell me your name. Right now I'm going to go inside." Amber stood up. "Be careful next time, okay."

The boy nodded then headed down the steps. He paused on the sidewalk and turned back to face them. "It's Tobb," he blurted out then raced toward the barn.

Amber chuckled. "He's going to be a firecracker."

"Going to be?" Chase grunted. "I have a feeling he's on his way now. His mother did good getting him here."

"Yes, she did. Getting him here before it's too late. Did you see that fading bruise on his jaw?" Her voice grated and her own jaw was rigid.

"I saw it." He could feel the tension radiating from her even though there was a foot between them. No kid should have to go through what Tobb had obviously been through but looking at Amber it almost seemed personal to her. What had happened to her? He was almost certain there was something in her past that pushed her. Had she been abused? Or had someone dear to her gone through this? Chase planned to find out.

"Tobb." The screen door opened again and Dottie came onto the porch. Tall, dark headed and elegant she stopped short when she saw them. "Oh hello. I didn't know we had company. Sorry but did a cute little guy about so high run past you?" She held her hand hip high.

"Tobb went toward the barn," Chase said.

"Oh then he's fine. He's crazy for the new foal

we have out there. I'll go get him in a minute. It's good to see you again. Hi, Chase," she held out her hand to Amber and shook momentarily. "And I'm Amber Rivers, Sadie's friend. I saw you at the wedding but it was a little crazy and I didn't get to meet you."

Dottie chuckled. "There were a lot of people there. I'm so happy for them. But, Brady told me about you and your job with the help lines."

Chase watched the two get to know each other as Amber told Dottie what she did. When Dottie invited them to come in he glanced toward the barn.

"You know what, y'all don't need me in there. I just came to show Amber where the ranch was so I think I'll go check on Tobb. Would that be a help to you, Dottie?"

"That would be great. The truth is right now there are no other boys here and the little girls are all playing dolls in the playroom and he's bored. A cowboy to talk to might be exactly what he needs."

"Then no hurry y'all have a good visit and I'll see if I can teach Tobb how to brush a horse down or something."

Relief lit Dottie's expression and Amber smiled at him and he felt it all the way through him like a light beam slicing through darkness… Turning away he headed toward the barn and could only wonder why that smile of hers affected him so strongly.

Amber followed Dottie into the shelter and after showing her the house with its large open rooms and introducing her to a few of the ladies who were living there. Esther Mae was sitting in a rocking chair in the nursery rocking a baby. When she saw Amber she beamed a brilliant smile at her.

"So glad you made it, Amber," she said in a hushed voice.

"I'm glad I came. You look like you have a great job this morning."

"Oh, I do," Esther Mae cooed then winked at Amber and Dottie. "It does my heart good to hold a baby."

Amber was touched by Esther Mae's giving spirit. These families had been through a lot and love was what they need.

After a moment they moved on and went back to the kitchen, grabbed glasses of tea and Dottie led her to her office. It was a large room that she explained had been Brady's daddy's office. It was now a female domain with soft blue walls above the dark wood wainscoting on the lower half of the walls. It had red chairs and gray rugs. Accents drew all the colors together and made it a happy, yet, elegant room.

Amber sat down in one of the chairs and Dottie did too choosing not to sit behind the desk. Since this was not a business meeting that made sense to Amber—though she suddenly realized that she was interested in knowing what kind of position Dottie was filling for the shelter.

That was unexpected too. Why would she even be considering such an idea?

"So how did you get involved with having a shelter," she asked, her curiosity getting the better of her.

"It's a long story but I lived in Florida and my home collapsed on top of me during a hurricane. I was badly injured, nearly died actually and after the months and months of rehab I knew I wanted to do something worthwhile with my life. I had changed during that time. I was a candy maker and my brother was involved in a women's shelter in California. So that's where the idea came from. I was crossing the country heading that way and I got stranded here in Mule Hollow. It was...the most wonderful experience of my life. And God's perfect plan. Needless to say some other things transpired and I ended up with Brady—which was the blessing of my life—and the shelter ended up here. It's wonderful and exciting. And fulfilling in so many ways." She looked thoughtful. "I thought I had my life all mapped out and figured out and when I look back at what transpired to get me here it was so very clear that I wasn't in control after all. That a plan was already in place that put me exactly where I was supposed to be."

"That is so cool. I may want the full details one day though."

Dottie chuckled. "Oh, it's quiet a story but I don't want to just talk about me right now. I'd like to know about your work."

Amber took a sip of her tea, trying to settle the unease that had suddenly filled her thinking about the problems surrounding her back home. "I answer the phone at the hotline. I'm the first contact for a woman reaching out for help. It's a stressful job sometimes because I take it entirely too seriously. There have been times when I can't get the woman to trust me…she hangs up before any connection to her is made and I never hear from her again. That kills me—I, I wonder often what becomes of those women. But I focus on the ones who I can get to take the next step in the process. The ones I can help pull from the waves." She often felt like a lifeguard. And she didn't like losing a victim.

"I'm sure that has to be hard when someone doesn't carry through with the call for help."

"The stress of that, of when I lose one often threatens to pull me beneath the waves…if I don't pull back and focus on cases I've won I'd be torn up all the time. The lives they saved through the program are what keep me going."

And it was true.

Dottie was studying her. "Have you ever thought about coming on this end of the rescue process? Working with the ones who've made the choice…it's just as challenging but in a different way. We actually have a really good success rate, our women don't go back…we lose a few but we have more who learn skills in the workplace that enable them to provide for themselves and their kids. Many have even fallen for local cowboys and stayed here. Lynn for instance, I don't know if you met her but she's married to Chance, the pastor who married Sadie and Rafe."

"Oh, I did meet her briefly. She was busy with

their twins and the younger little girl so we didn't get to do much more than be introduced."

"They keep her busy. But there are several who live here and thrive and several who come yearly to our reunion. We're holding one this weekend at the Wells'place. You should come."

"Oh we are coming to that." Amber liked the idea of a reunion. After that she listened with great interest to what Dottie had to say and asked a few questions but she knew she couldn't do this. Knew that she wasn't made for small town life and that if she chose something like this she would feel like she was abandoning the frontline. And it was just something she didn't think she could ever do.

Could she?

"Hey there, Tobb," Chase said as he entered the barn. The kid was sitting on a hay bale watching the colt inside the stall. It was a beautiful colt a deep chestnut with long legs and a nice head on it. The colt nickered when he entered. Tobb watched Chase with wary eyes but didn't say anything. Chase leaned against the stall gate and held his hand out to the colt. It moved toward him and he scratched the colt between the eyes. "You can pet him."

Tobb shook his head.

"He's tame. Come on."

The boy eased off the hay bale and walked to the wooden gate. He slipped his hand in and touched the colt without hesitation. Chase thought it was more of an action the kid was making to prove to him that he wasn't afraid rather than to enjoy it.

"See not so bad is it?" he asked.

The kid shrugged but he kept his hand on the colt and gently ran his hand from the colt's forehead to his nose and then again.

Chase didn't press, he just let the kid get to know the colt. He knew that Brady kept gentle colts here just for this purpose. Kids were infatuated with the beautiful animals. And many times the women who came here, whether they had children or not loved to come and watch or pet the horses that were kept in the pastures around the home. There was something to be said about quiet contemplation and beauty mixed together. And then again watching a cute colt or a beautiful horse was just a pleasurable thing no matter who you were.

After a minute the kid looked up at him. "He

likes me," he said, and there was a smile on his face that got Chase right in the gut.

"Yeah, he does. Did you know a horse is a good judge of character? They know when a person has good intentions. Now of course if they aren't broke yet it's not always easy to get close to them because their natural instinct is to run, running is a horse's God given defense mechanism. It's all they have in way of staying safe from predators. So until they're gentled you can't hold wariness against them." Chase couldn't help thinking that statement could apply to a kid who had been through what this kid had probably been through. The wariness in his body language reminded Chase of a colt learning to trust rather than run. Tobb pulled his hand back and stared at the colt as it nickered wanting to be petted again.

"That's all it can do is run?"

"It can kick and buck but its first instinct is to get away from danger. Even for kids and adults sometimes running away is the best thing. You need to get out of the danger zone."

The kid nodded. "Yeah, sometimes being a kid stinks. My mom's boyfriend hit her...a lot and she just always told me to run."

Chase tensed and tried not to show the anger

flaring inside of him. "Did you? At your age that's all you could do."

Tobb nodded and his lip trembled. "But if I'd been bigger I'd have kicked and bucked and I'd have made him pay for hurting my mom."

Chase laid a hand on Tobb's shoulder. "You did what you had to do and your mom has come here for help. It's a good thing. A man shouldn't ever raise a hand to a woman or a kid and when possible he needs to find a better way of dealing with conflict with a way that doesn't involve fighting." Chase was sure not to say always because the truth was sometimes a man just had to fight. Running wasn't always an option.

Tobb didn't look convinced but he nodded. "My mom said he wasn't a man and she didn't want him ever hurting me so she knew she had to get us away."

"She was right."

"Do you think I could learn to ride a horse?"

The change of subject threw Chase but then, maybe a kid processed things that way. He really didn't know much about kids other than he had been one once but that seemed like a long time ago to Chase. "Yeah, sure you could. You can talk to Mr. and Mrs. Cannon and find out if they will teach you how to ride here, if not you can come to my ranch and we'll teach you."

"Really…awesome." Tobb grinned and actually jumped with excitement.

Chase hadn't ever thought about it before but suddenly the idea of helping a kid or some kids learn to ride sounded like a good plan. He knew that Lilly and Cort Wells had some kind of program at their horse ranch that might accommodate this but this appealed to him and he wanted to do it.

CHAPTER FOURTEEN

"That was sweet of you to spend time with Tobb," Amber said a few seconds after they'd started back down the drive from the shelter. She'd been impressed when Chase and Tobb had walked back up to the house from the barn and Tobb had informed Dottie that Chase was going to teach him to ride. Chase had quickly added that it would be only after Tobb's mother and Dottie had decided it was okay.

"I didn't offer to be sweet. The boy was hurting and he asked about riding. I've never thought about it before so it feels like I'm actually running behind the curve on this. I should have thought about offering some lessons to the kids here before."

Amber studied him. "I think you're being a little hard on yourself. It's not something that just jumps out at you as a needed service." She was realizing that Chase took responsibility to a higher level. She was drawn to that. Since her dad had taken no responsibility she found Chase's character and drive to be a major...attraction. She'd leave it at that.

"Now I know about it and I can do something about it," he was saying as she pulled her attention back to the discussion...and not thinking about Chase and how much she was beginning to respect him.

She smiled at him, liking so much the way he thought. Her phone rang and she reached for it—this time she glanced at the ID. When she saw Jill, her co-worker's name a sense of dread filled her.

"I'm sorry I think I need to take this." She hit the answer button and placed it to her ear.

Chase's brows knit as he watched her and she wondered if he was reading the tension in her expression that she was fairly certain was showing.

"Hey, Jill."

"Amber! I'm so glad you answered. I can't believe it—"

She was rattled, terribly rattled and Amber instantly froze. "What happened?"

"That crazy man broke in here and destroyed your desk area. He ripped things apart and went through everything. And..." she paused and Amber's heart dropped to her stomach.

"What else," she asked. "Did he hurt you?"

"No. I wasn't here. But, your desk calendar, where you'd scribbled Sadie's wedding date down and the ranch's address...it's gone. He took it. The whole thing."

A chill settled on Amber like she'd been doused with ice water.

He was coming to Mule Hollow.

"What's wrong?" Chase asked.

Amber gripped the phone and forced herself to calm down. "Is that everything?"

Her friend's voice trembled as she said that was everything. "The police are looking for him. But Amber he's crazy. They know who he is and he keeps doing this. It's like he's so mad at you that he no longer cares. I think he wants to harm you and doesn't care about what happens to him afterward."

That wasn't helping Amber at the moment. After few minutes she hung up and finally met Chase's gaze. He'd pulled the truck over on the side of the road next to a pasture full of cattle. He'd been silent after she hadn't answered his first question. Now however, his eyes bore into her.

"Talk to me."

Amber couldn't sit still. She couldn't explain the mixture of emotions that drove her from the interior of the truck. Pushing open the door she exited the truck. The tall grass on the shoulder of the road reached her calves as she stalked to the end of the truck and moved to the edge of the pavement. She kept on walking, too frustrated to think straight.

"Amber, hold on." Chase jogged to catch up. "Stop. Talk to me."

She spun around. "Talbert broke into the call office and tore up my desk area. He took the calendar that I'd written the ranch address on and the date. He knows I'm here." She ran both hands through her hair, trying to process in her own mind that this man was really willing to ruin his life to get at her. "I guess I've been in denial. This man has lost it. And he really hates me."

Rage hardened Chase's eyes as he took the information in. His voice was steady when he spoke, "We'll go see Brady again. This is going to be okay. I won't let anything happen to you."

Amber took a deep breath. She wanted to say she could take care of herself but she held back because at the moment she was in such shock that the guy was really stalking her that she wasn't convinced she could take care of anything. "I, I'm fine."

"You don't look fine. You're white as a sheet."

"I just need to process this."

Chase was standing close to her and suddenly he reached out and pulled her into his arms and just held her against him. She went, needing the feel of his strong arms and not even realizing how much until she was there. She trembled and her arms slowly lifted and went around his waist. She just held on.

"Thank you," she said.

He nodded against her hair. "You looked like you could use a hug."

"It doesn't mean I'm going to fall apart. This is as apart as I'm going to go," she said, her voice muffled against his shoulder. He smelled so good, so masculine. She let her defenses down and for just a moment let him take all of her burden while she just held on to him.

They didn't move for the longest time as if he understood she needed only his support.

And then he kissed her temple. "I'm not going to let anything happen to you, Amber," he said drawing her to look up at him.

157

Their faces were so close and for a moment she thought he was going to kiss her...

Chase's heart pounded as he looked down at Amber. His arms tightened and he lowered his head—just before his lips met hers he stopped himself. What was he doing? She needed encouragement and support right now.

"Amber, you're a strong woman. You're going to get past this and Talbert's going to be behind bars for a very long time."

"I hope so, not just for myself but for his girlfriend—ex-girlfriend."

"Right. Are you alright now?"

She nodded. "Thanks for your support." She let go of his waist and stepped out of his arms. "I'm a little shook up. I'll admit it. I've never had a stalker before and I'm not a big fan but I'm done having my meltdown."

He grinned, loving the grit in her words. "There you go. Let me see that spunk."

"It's not that I'm afraid—I mean, I know I can take care of myself. But I'm also aware that I'm not superwoman."

Chase gave her shoulder a gentle squeeze.

"Let's go see Brady and Zane. Both are extremely good at their jobs. This lowlife might come to Mule Hollow but I can assure you it won't be exactly what he's expecting. I want to make certain they know there might be trouble and it might be soon. Everything is going to be alright. I promise."

She nodded and his heart squeezed tight as he made himself head toward the truck...what he wanted to do was pull her back into his arms and explore the feelings that were tangled inside of him. But that would come later.

Right now he had a promise to keep.

Brady had been a cop in LA and Zane had been a Texas Ranger. Both had opted for a small town life with the women they loved. Mule Hollow had benefited from their choice by now having one of the finest law enforcement divisions around. Amber was impressed with the information that Chase had given her on the way back into town. She knew that informing her of their credentials was his way of quietly reassuring her, without just blurting it out, that she needn't be afraid. She was in capable hands.

That was the thing...she'd never thought she

was in bad hands because, after all, Chase was watching over her and she'd learned through watching everything else that he did that Chase Hartley was capable in every sense of the word.

"We have a picture of him," Brady said a few minutes later after they'd entered his office and told him what they'd learned. "I just got off the phone with the detective working your case."

Zane, who had been introduced, had his arms crossed and one shoulder leaned against the wall as he listened. He was a very attractive man in a rugged way with chiseled features and a powerful build. "He's coming, we know that. He wouldn't have taken that calendar, we don't believe, if he didn't have plans to at least check you out. From a distance or for an altercation of some manner. Either way, we don't plan to let him get close to you."

"Chase," Brady said. "You're planning to stay close to her, right?"

"I plan on it. He'll have to come through me to get near her…and that's not going to happen."

The look of concern…of care in Chase's gaze had her pulse spiking, but the gravel in his voice tugged at her heart like nothing she'd ever experienced. He was standing up for her as were

Brady and Zane but she could tell that for Chase this had turned personal…and that put Amber into territory she'd never been before.

She had to force herself to focus and reaffirm her own strength, to stand up for herself and be counted. "I'm here, guys," she said rising from the chair she was sitting in and moved across the room and faced them. She couldn't let them take over. She had to be a part of her own protection. "I thank y'all for what you are doing, but I'm in on this too. I have a say in what happens to me."

They all looked at her with what…curious expressions maybe? She frowned. "I do know self-defense which means I'm not helpless and I refuse to be treated as if I am." She was beginning to sound like a broken record but doggone it they weren't listening. And at this point she needed to remind herself that she was not helpless. Though she kept thinking about Chase's arms around her and she had to admit that it felt good to know he was determined to take care of her, she still had to remain true to herself.

"And that's a great thing," Brady said. "But you also have to remember that this is our town. Our county. We're responsible and Zane and I plan to keep you and everyone in our jurisdiction safe.

That makes this and you our business. So you'll just have to bear with us."

"Of course I will and I appreciate what y'all are doing for me. I can't believe this guy would take the time to come after me like this."

"Some people can't be figured out," Chase said.

"You've taken something this man valued," Zane added. "He might have abused his girlfriend but you helped her leave, so the question is how upset has that made him? A lot if his tracking you is an indication and he's extremely dangerous."

"I'm feeling kind of dangerous myself at the moment. I'll make a stand and draw this man out before I have my life disrupted much more."

All eyes were on her. Her stomach churned and her palms itched, but it was true. "I will not let this bully keep me in hiding for much longer."

"I'm going to go stir crazy if I have to sit around too long," Amber informed Chase as they drove back to the ranch."

She'd been quiet most of the ride and he'd been preoccupied with thoughts of securing the ranch, which was pretty secure with all of his partners and the ranch hands too. Once he alerted everyone to the threat he felt reasonably certain she would be safe, but he wasn't taking anything for granted. He'd make sure everyone knew what Ned Talbert looked like and Brady was doing the same in town with a handful of people he knew would be on the lookout. That included Norma Sue, Adela and Esther Mae. But it also included Sam at the diner and App and Stanley. Those two sat in the front window of the diner from daybreak till sometimes after lunch playing checkers, poking jabs at each other and anyone who'd listen as they kept tabs on everything going on around them. If Ned stepped foot in Mule Hollow when those two were around he was toast. On that end Chase believed he could relax because those two and Sam also took being retired vets seriously. They'd be on a mission to keep Amber safe and he knew it. So did Brady and Zane.

And he wasn't ever going to think about what the women were going to do. Lacy and Sheri over at the salon would be alerted too. He told Amber this and she gasped.

"They'll help?"

"Sure they will. They'll have your back. That's what Mule Hollow folks do. You're not in this alone."

"I don't want anyone getting hurt. Do you think it's wise to show them his picture? We know what he's capable of."

"They'll be fine. They run in packs," he grinned despite his worry for her. He could tell she was alarmed but she wasn't letting it paralyze her. She was fighting back and he liked that but he also worried that it could get her into trouble. And on a personal note he knew he didn't want that to happen.

If he got any more distracted by her he might have a problem…but everything about her distracted him. The way she looked, the way she smelled—a soft low profile scent of sweet that was starting to drive him a little nuts. The way her jaw stiffened when she was feeling challenged—he liked it and it made him smile as he glanced over at her.

He liked her concern for others over herself.

She was staring out the window and her knee was moving as she tapped her foot on the floorboard. He had a feeling she wasn't even aware she was doing it and he wondered if it was nerves or that she did it when she was deep in thought. Either way, it was a sign that things had shifted and she knew she was facing something serious.

He wasn't kidding himself, he knew he had his work cut out for him keeping her close. She truly believed she could take care of herself and maybe she could...he just didn't plan on finding that out. He wanted Ned taken care of before he got anywhere near Amber.

CHAPTER SIXTEEN

The wind was out of the north as they drove toward the benefit that evening and Amber hoped it didn't get too cold and mess the evening up.

Lilly and Cort Wells were horse trainers who lived on the other side of Mule Hollow. Along with their horse business they held retreats for youth groups and worked with many organizations on introducing kids to ranch life who wouldn't normally have access to country life, cattle or horses.

Tonight they were hosting the Thanksgiving Reunion for No Place Like Home and making their ranch available to those whose life had been touched and helped by the refuge. Those who supported the home were also invited. Amber had been thrilled when Chase hadn't tried to keep her from coming.

"I'm sticking to you like glue," he'd said. "But I can't think of a safer place other than our ranch for you to be. Everyone will be there."

He'd been right. The place was packed as they drove through the gates and parked along the driveway. Amber could see the house and the stables a good distance up the lane and felt a sense of excitement as she exited the truck and met Chase on the driveway. This was going to be fun.

She was startled when a small gray donkey came trotting down the middle of the driveway. The little donkey or burro had huge brown eyes that were lit with curiosity.

"Oh my goodness," Amber exclaimed spying the curious burro as it pranced toward them. When it was just a few feet away it halted, sat down on its hunches, rolled its huge protruding lips back, exposing big white teeth as it studied them with inquisitive eyes.

"How adorable, she's smiling at us." Amber just wanted to run over and give the funny animal a hug.

Chase grinned. "Amber, meet Samantha the most mischievous donkey you'll ever meet. I'm assuming she is the welcoming committee tonight. She loves the activity that goes on around here."

As soon as he said it a group of young kids came running down the driveway, their cheeks red from running and playing.

"Samantha," they called, and giggles erupted as they reached Samantha.

Amber laughed when the donkey tossed her head back and let out the most awful he-haw in the history of the world. "Oh my," Amber chuckled. "She's got a set of lungs on her."

"Hey, lady," a young girl with red pigtails said, scrunching her face as she spoke. "You mind if we get Samantha to play with us. She likes to play hide and seek."

"I don't mind but I think you need to ask Samantha that question. It looks like she does what she wants to do."

The girl got a very serious look on her face. "Yes, ma'am," she said then turned to the other three kids behind her and held up her hands. "We need to ask Samantha," she said in a very adult voice. All of them nodded and turned toward the donkey who was now relaxing on the opposite hip than she had been and somewhere during the conversation she'd plucked a piece of grass from the ground and was now chewing on it. Big brown eyes laced with long fringe eyelashes looked back at the kids. She flopped her tail, the fringe on the end of it slapping soundlessly on the drive.

"Samantha," the girl said. "Would you wanna play?"

Amber glanced at Chase and he winked at her, sending her stomach fluttering. She pulled her gaze away from his and back to the kids.

Samantha leaned forward and gently nudged the little girl's shoulder making her giggle. At that moment the other kids started giggling too and clamoring close so the donkey would nudge them. Giggles erupted as each received a nudge and then like lightening Samantha sprang to her feet, let out a gosh-awful sound and pranced back toward the barns with the kids trailing her.

Amber's hand automatically went over her heart as she laughed. "That was great."

"Yeah, I forgot to mention the number one attraction is Samantha the donkey. That little gal lights up anybody's day."

"I love it. Oh, Chase, I'm truly excited about tonight." She started walking and Chase fell into step beside her.

"It should be fun. They've got games and hayrides planned and a campfire. Then there is some supervised horseback riding in the round pen too. And I think more but that's what I can think of. And of course Samantha."

She smiled. "It's such a great idea. I've been trying to figure out all afternoon why I'm so thrilled to be here and I've finally understood. I don't ever get to see this side of a family's journey from abuse to happy. Those children's happy faces did my heart good. So good."

She paused and let the thought sink in. Chase halted too.

"That would be hard I would think. Helping all those families but never seeing the journey after your initial contact."

"I never really thought about it a lot until recently and it's been on my mind some ever since learning about reunion. I totally get it being a Thanksgiving Reunion." Her eyes teared up.

"Are you okay?"

She nodded. "I am. I'm...just a little overwhelmed."

"You're going through a lot right now. Most people would be falling apart, Amber, and you're rock solid. Too rock solid. I worry. It's okay to let your guard down you know."

He'd taken the conversation back to Ned. Back to her being stalked. "I don't want to go there right now, okay. I want to go see these families. I want to see the end result of what I've worked so hard at for all these years. I want to see happiness and freedom from the abuse and hardship these families found after they made that call."

Chase draped an arm around her shoulders and pulled her close for a quick hug. "I have a feeling you may be smiling more than the kids tonight."

His strength and support flowed through her. "Chase, thank you. I'm glad I came with you."

His eyes crinkled at the edges. "Believe me it's my pleasure."

Amber forced herself to move away from him and start toward the house. If she wasn't so excited about the reunion she could have stood there all evening. Maybe forever…

The thought blindsided her.

A northern had moved in making the evening really pleasant. Chase watched the kids running from huge jumping toys to stick horse races. He'd spent a lot of the evening moving around visiting with friends and trying to not hover around Amber. He stayed close but tried to give her some room. Brady was there and they talked some more as both of them remained alert, ready for anything.

When Chase spotted Tobb playing with a group of boys he was pleased to see the kid having a good time. Almost automatically his gaze shifted back to Amber.

It took a special kind of woman to dedicate her life to hearing these stories and helping them leave to find safety and happiness.

He wanted to talk to her more, find out everything about her. He wanted to find out more about how she felt, how she endured and what drove her to get up every day and hear more sad stories. What from her past drove her, because he felt certain there was something.

"She sure is a purdy little gal," App boomed behind him and Chase very nearly jumped out of his skin.

"Hey, App, you need to give a little warning before you sneak up on a man."

App's wrinkled face lifted in a grin. "I wouldn't get to see you jump if I did that. You were so caught up mooning over Amber thar you wouldn't have seen me if I'd walked straight up to you."

"So you got me on that." Chase couldn't deny it. "She's an amazing woman."

"I thought you had that look in yor eye."

Chase realized anyone from a mile away could hear everything App was saying.

"I'm just looking out for her," he said.

"Yup. And that's why I came over. Me and Stanley are on the lookout. Sam too. If we see anything, and I mean ANYTHING suspicious or lookin' like at feller, disguised or otherwise you can bet we'll be alerting everyone."

"App, maybe we need to try and keep this on the quiet."

"That's the truth," Norma Sue said coming up to them. "App, I could hear you spoutin' off all the way over at the food table. You need to wear your hearing aids."

App looked concerned and spoke softer, "I tell ya, I forget I talk loud. I can't hardly hear a lick of what I'm saying right now. And I hate them thar aids. Worthless noise magnifiers."

"I know and I feel for you but remember we can hear you just fine when you talk low," Norma said. "The thing is, we're all on the lookout and we're ready. When Brady came around with that picture today we were all at the diner and we all agreed this coward shows up he's going to get more than he's bargained for."

Chase grinned despite the seriousness of the

issue. "You all just be careful. I'm sure Brady told you to take no risks."

Norma hiked a brow. "Oh he told us alright. You leave our wellbeing to us. We might be old but we've been around the block a few times and we can take care of ourselves."

Chase spent the next little while wondering what exactly Norma Sue was talking about. He decided he might need to mention it to Brady and Zane. There was no telling what kind of trouble the matchmakers and the checker players were going to get themselves into protecting Amber.

Amber had gotten with Dottie and Lacy the minute she arrived to find out how she could help. They'd introduced her to Lilly Wells who was hosting the night along with her husband Cort. The group also included Sheri and her very dry sense of humor.

"So," Sheri drawled, cuddling her adorable, baby boy in her arms. "You've got trouble we hear."

Everyone already knew? Brady and Zane hadn't wasted any time sending out their alerts. She hadn't come here to discuss Ned Talbert. "Maybe but it's going to be okay."

"Well if he makes the mistake of showing up in town asking questions someone is going to see him and send out the alert. Just thought you should know that. We understand what you do for a living and we plan to protect you however we can."

"See all these kiddos," Lacy said. "And these smiling faced women walking around here. Many of them are a direct result of someone at the call centers picking up the phone and saying the words they needed to hear that gave them the courage to make the break. It brings me to tears thinking about it. And you're one of those angels on the end of that phone line."

Amber's heart pounded and she felt so many kindred spirits as she looked around the group of smiling supporters. She blinked back the sudden threat of tears. No wonder both Sadie and Maddie had such wonderful things to say about the town. About the people.

"Thank y'all for your support. It is unexpected but appreciated."

Lilly smiled at her, a really sweet smile. "I don't know why you say unexpected. That's what we do around here. We support each other."

"I'm beginning to understand that." Amber

looked around the group and felt joy at what Sadie had found here. Not just a husband but a community too. Amber was looking forward to seeing her friend when she arrived back home tomorrow. And when Amber headed back to her own life, as soon as the stalker issue was resolved, she would know that her friend had everything here she needed to start her new life.

As the evening progressed everyone climbed onto two large trailers loaded with hay. The men made sure all the kids were settled on the hay and no standing up was allowed. Adults then settled in with the kids and the hayride began. Amber found a spot beside Esther Mae in the corner of one of the trailers.

"This does bring back some memories of me and my Hank in our younger years. Hayrides used to be a big thing in our day." Esther Mae chuckled. "Snuggling up with your sweetie on a chilly evening..." She sighed. "Those were the days."

Amber had developed a tender spot for the redhead, despite her over the top desire to marry off every single person within miles around her. She had a good heart.

"It sounds like a lot of fun," she said, her thoughts instantly shifting to snuggling with Chase.

"Oh it was. And speaking of snuggling here comes Chase. Yoo-hoo, Chase," she called as he hopped onto the trailer and glanced around. "Over here."

"Hey, ladies," he greeted them as he eased through the kids.

Esther Mae popped up out of her seat. "Hey there yourself, cowboy. Take my seat. I just remembered I was supposed to ride on the other trailer with Norma Sue. My Hank is driving the tractor of that one." And with that said, she grabbed Chase's arm and tugged him past her then pushed him into the hay beside Amber.

Amber gasped when Chase plunked down beside her. He was laughing too as they both watched the spunky matchmaker sashay through the masses and hightailing it off the trailer.

"Well, that was a pretty obvious setup," Chase drawled. "Norma Sue sent me over here said I was supposed to ride shotgun on this trailer. Now I know." He laughed and shook his head. "I planned to ride the one you were on anyways so their obvious matchmaking wasn't even needed."

She was smiling and a thrill of gladness had hit her the moment Chase hopped onto the trailer. Now that he was squeezed in beside her she couldn't get the smile off her face. Especially after Esther Mae's antics.

"I hope you don't mind if I join you?"

"No," she choked out on a chuckle. "Not at all." Her heart was racing at his nearness and the feel of his thigh pressing against hers. He placed a hand behind her on the hay bale and suddenly she felt like she was sitting in the crook of his arm though they weren't touching…but if she leaned back just a little she would be. The thought made her pulse jump. She looked up into his eyes and he was watching her.

"I'm glad to see you were able to relax tonight." He leaned close so she could hear him over the laughter of the kids.

"It's been nice." The trailer hit a bump sending everyone bouncing and she fell against Chase. His arm instantly came around her, holding her steady.

"A little rough there," he drawled against her ear sending a tingle of awareness coursing through her.

Her hand had come to rest on his chest as she steadied herself and when she looked up smiling, they were very near. Her breath shortened and she was very aware that she wanted to kiss Chase Hartley. But she was also just as aware that they were surrounded by kids and this was not the place nor the time to be thinking about the feel of his lips on hers.

"Amber," he said softly. "You are beautiful. Inside and out."

Her heart lunged in her chest. *This was not the place. Not the place.*

"Thank you," she said and then forced herself to pull away from him. But for the rest of the evening everything about Chase held her captive. And suddenly small town life began to look extraordinarily appealing.

CHAPTER SEVENTEEN

It was ten o'clock when they reached the ranch. Chase had been quiet on the drive home. He'd been quiet most of the evening after the hayride. But then so had she. Amber had become distracted by thoughts of Chase and she'd found her gaze seeking him out across the campfire. And each time she'd found him his gaze had sought her too.

There was something about him that called to her. Maybe it was his dedication and desire to keep her safe that pulled at her. Or just the fact that she found him so crazily attractive and so very kind.

There had been handsome cowboys swarming all over that shindig tonight and none of them had drawn her, made her long to be near them or long for even one kiss. She'd thought about kissing Chase all night.

That thought had her preoccupied all the way home.

This was all wrong. She loved her city life, her career, her fast paced lifestyle. She'd come to appreciate the country more during this week than she'd thought possible but could she adjust to it?

"Amber, who hurt you?"

His question came out of nowhere and took her completely by surprise. She didn't make a secret of the fact that her dad hadn't been dad of the year material but she also didn't talk about him. "What makes you think someone hurt me?" she asked, curious as to why he sounded so sure of the question.

The chill was still in the air and she pulled her lightweight jacket tight around her.

"Because I've been watching and you're just so determined to help. And I was listening to you talking to Tobb's mother near the campfire right before we headed back to the house. You don't just understand, you get it and the women you talk to feel that. They're drawn to you once they realize you've been there."

"I've never told anyone I've been there."

"But they get it and know it even without you admitting it."

"Just like you."

He nodded and touched her cheek. They were

standing on the patio in the beam of the porch light. "I can't stand the thought of someone hurting you."

She didn't want to talk about this but... "My dad was abusive. My mom, she loved him and kept believing he would get help and be better. But he refused to go and then one night he hit me...the next day he left."

She saw the anger flash in Chase's eyes and felt the tension even though they weren't touching. "I'm sorry you had to live through that. Are you alright now?"

His care touched her. She could visibly see how much he hated that she'd had abuse in her past. "I'm fine. I learned to fill the void left in the wake of a deadbeat dad. I learned to deal with the wish that I could have had a regular dad...and I've made peace with the fact that my mother didn't get me out of the situation."

He shook his head. "That's got to be hard. But you seem to have a good relationship now."

"We do. She apologized and apologized for putting her love for him over my safety. For years she punished herself for putting me in danger and she wouldn't allow herself to be forgiven. But eventually once she realized I was okay she gave herself grace and let it go."

"Look, I know the guys are going to be coming back home any minute and this conversation is going to get interrupted. And I'm not ready for it to end. Would you want to go for a horseback ride?"

"At night?"

He nodded. "It's great. And tonight with the moon so big and bright it'll be amazing."

Amber thought he was amazing and the idea was so tempting...she knew she should say no. "Yes, it sounds...fun." She knew she should go inside. Let the night be over and hope that tomorrow she was thinking straight again. But tonight all she wanted was to spend more time with Chase.

He took her hand and her pulse raced.

"You're going to like it. But I want to continue this conversation. I want to know all about you, Amber."

It had been a long time since anyone had truly wanted to know about her. At least anyone who she was willing to share with...and she felt comfortable sharing this with Chase. She trusted him. Besides her mother and Sadie no one knew this much about her past.

As Chase saddled Nugget he had to fight the anger twisting in his gut. To imagine someone raising a hand to Amber undid him. He'd known it, felt certain of it, but until she'd actually admitted it he hadn't let the anger surge. But now, it was all he could do to keep his hands from shaking as he cinched the saddle up.

And her mother...her mother had let herself be abused in the hopes that he would get better. She'd put her child at risk *for a man*. He couldn't fathom it. Couldn't understand and as far as he was concerned there was nothing to understand. A man who would do such a thing to a woman and child was not a man. It was black and white. And Amber or any child should have come first. When the abuse started Amber's mother should have reached out for help.

Should have reached out to someone like Amber on the other end of a thousand hotlines out there for help.

He could understand that some women might be afraid. But Amber's mother didn't sound like she was afraid. She just didn't do it.

He pushed the thought away, needing to calm

down before he tried to speak any more. It was a beautiful night and he was driven tonight to just show Amber that all men weren't out to harm her.

"I think this is the most beautiful horse I've ever seen. Seeing you riding him over that hill that first day took my breath away."

Her words brought him back from his deep thoughts. He grinned. "What about the rider?" he couldn't help asking. She laughed and he loved hearing it.

"It was the whole package. You're a very good rider."

"If it helps me impress you then that's all that I care about." He winked, and was glad to see her smile again.

He put a boot in the stirrup and took the saddle in one smooth move he'd done a thousand times. Once in the saddle he held a hand down to her. She had a baffled expression.

"But, I thought—"

"Wrong. I thought we could ride together." He was afraid she would refuse but then she placed her hand in his and he tugged her up so she could get her foot in the stirrup and then hop onto the horse behind him. "Now hang on to me. I don't want you falling off."

She answered him by bringing her arms around his waist. He covered her hands with his own and the moment felt right. Everything about the two of them together felt right.

The moon cast a glow across the pastures and a dreamy state over Amber's heart. Riding like this with Chase felt as if it was right. They rode in silence for the longest time, following the shimmering trail of the moonlight through the pasture, heading toward a horizon on a hill where the moon seemed to be just an arm's length above the ground. Amber was washed in a peace that she'd never felt before. As if God had lain this night out just for her. It was so perfect.

She let everything fade to the background: her past, her stalker, her future. She just let the beauty and perfection of this perfect gift flow in a wave over her, washing everything else away.

"Are you alright back there," Chase asked as they were riding up the hillside.

"I'm good. Just marveling how gorgeous it is tonight. Thank you for thinking of this. The moon was nowhere near this gorgeous at the hayride."

"It had only just begun to rise then."

When they reached the top of the hill Amber gasped at the valley bathed in moonlight before them and behind them. "You knew this is what I'd see. Oh, Chase...talk about romantic."

Even as the word was out of her mouth she wished for it back. Because it was romantic and the fact that she was here with Chase made it all the more true.

"I thought you'd like it. I enjoy riding at night. There's a peace to it that settles me. And I hoped it could do that same thing for you."

She was touched by him. She'd never been around a man who took such care to please her. To show her beauty like this. Amber knew it had only been a week since she'd met Chase but there was something powerful going on between them.

"Let's get down for a few minutes," he said, then rounded his right leg over Nuggets head and hopped to the ground.

He turned back to her and wrapped his hands around her waist then lifted her from the saddle. Her hands were on his shoulders as he lowered her to the ground. Her blood was rushing through her veins as her feet finally touched the ground in front of him.

His eyes bore into hers and she shivered with a

longing that went deep, into a part of her heart that she'd closed off so long ago that she hadn't even realized it.

Sadie had often said she didn't let men get close to her heart. That she didn't trust them. And that was because her father had hurt her with his abuse, but more from his total let down as a good father.

"Amber I have to confess that I brought you here because I wanted to share it with you. I was so angry back there at the house when you told me about your dad that I couldn't think straight. I wanted to show you something good. To express..." he tugged her a step closer to him and slowly, tenderly brushed hair from her temple. "No one should hurt you, Amber. You deserve so much more."

His words touched her and she wondered...what would it be like to be loved by this man? Loved...yes, physically but also to be loved with his heart. His soul. What would forever be like with Chase? *It would be wonderful.*

"I've only known you a week, Amber, but I've never felt this before. I'm falling for you and I can't believe or understand how it could be happening this fast but I want you to know how I feel. I want the opportunity to see where this could go."

She sucked in a deep breath, his scent filling her lungs. "It's so fast. I'm going back home when this is all over and I get the okay from the police." She was babbling when she knew she wanted to throw her arms around his neck and tell him she was all in. That she wanted to see where this was going too.

But she didn't. "I can't lie. I'm drawn to you, Chase. And so attracted to you. You're strong and kind and I feel so safe with you. But—"

"I get everything you're saying. But I'm just asking for a shot. I know we have a stalker to rid your life of, but then, I'm just asking for a shot."

He deserved a shot at...a relationship? A life with her? Amber wasn't sure how to classify what he deserved a shot at. But she knew that he deserved for her to take him seriously. He was putting everything on the line for her.

She nodded and tried to get control of her runaway heart rate. When he smiled and leaned down to kiss her she lifted on her tiptoes and met him. She didn't even fight to hold back.

The touch of his lips sent a warm wave of passion cascading over her, weakening her knees and igniting feelings inside of her she'd thought she'd never feel. Thought she would live without...her arms wrapped around his shoulders and drew him closer as she startled herself by joining in with the kiss. She let herself go in that moment, let everything go but loving Chase.

Love.

Her heart ached when he drew back. "Amber," he whispered against her lips. "You're one amazing woman." He kissed her again quickly then stepped back and took her hand in his and turned to stare up at the moon.

Amber couldn't begin to explain the emotions running through her. They stood there for the longest time not saying anything, just sharing the beauty of the night.

And after a while they climbed back on Nugget and made their way back along the moonlit trail.

Amber knew that that trail had led to her heart. But she couldn't believe or trust what she was feeling. Not this soon.

CHAPTER EIGHTEEN

Chase was in the kitchen with Ty and Dalton the next morning when Amber marched into the room punched her fist to her hips and declared she'd had enough.

All three of them stopped what they were doing and gave her their full attention.

"Enough of what?" he asked.

She glared. "Of this coward disrupting my life. Where is he? He's fallen off the face of the earth. He hasn't called, he hasn't shown up—what's he doing? Trying to drive me crazy? Well he's succeeded. I need space."

Ty glanced at Chase and so did Dalton who hiked a brow at him that pretty much said this is your rodeo. He stepped forward.

"Now, Amber, you know we're just waiting this out."

She shook her head. "Nope. I'm done waiting it

out. I want my life back. And I've thought about it all night long. He's going to call and he's going to call soon because it's been too long and I think he's here somewhere waiting to see me sweat."

That made sense. "Only I'm not sweating. We went to a party last night and then for a moonlit ride. And if he's watching then he's probably realizing that I don't go anywhere without an escort. Or without a crowd."

The moonlit ride comment had instantly gotten him more hiked brows but no words of interruption. He figured the chickens were scared to jump into the middle of a woman on a tirade.

He laid down the spatula that he'd been flipping bacon with and took a step toward her. "You might need to calm down," he wasn't sure what to do with a woman having a—well he wasn't sure what to call it. But he wasn't used to it and clueless about what to do for her.

"No, I don't need to sit down or calm down. I'm tired of waiting, Chase. I've called Sheriff Brady and told him to get ready because I'm coming to town. If y'all want to catch this dude as much as I do then we're going to throw him some bait. Me."

"No! We are not going to throw him some

bait."

"Oh yes I am. And you don't have any say in it, Chase."

His eyes narrowed. "Wanna bet? You just try to head out that door and get in your car without me..." What had happened between the time she'd gotten off Nugget and gone to bed and now?

"I'm going, Chase. I'm going to town at ten and I'm hanging out and you and Brady and Zane can figure out where you want to be but it won't be with me. I'm going to draw him out and then when he comes after me we'll get him."

"Not in a million years," he growled.

She glared up at him. "This is still my life and I'm an adult so yeah, this is the way it's going to be." They were toe to toe as he tried to intimidate her into letting go of this insane idea. But it didn't work. Even Ty and Dalton spoke up finally but she shot them down too.

"I'm doing this," she said. "Deal with it."

Amber had been too tempted by Chase out in the moonlight. She'd been ready to toss everything and fall into his arms and into his life. It was so unlike her. It didn't make sense and it scared her. Scared her far more than Ned Talbert.

She chalked it up to the fact that she needed her life back and she was going to get it. When ten o'clock rolled around she drove her little sports car into town and parked in front of Ashby's dress shop. Today she was going window shopping. Eating lunch with the girls at Sam's like she'd been planning to do all week and then she'd go check out Adela's apartment house that set at the end of Main Street. And if ole Ned didn't bite today she'd do it all over again tomorrow.

Chase had thrown a fit but in the end after Brady and Zane agreed that it was a way to bring him out. She knew they were all hiding out somewhere but she'd left that up to them.

She'd called in the troops and town was going to have just enough women to keep suspicions down.

She was getting out of her car when the posse came out of Pete's Feed and Seed and hurried toward her.

The posse came hustling across the street.

"Well, have you seen anything yet?" Esther Mae asked, leaning in close as she whispered. "I've got my big pink container of mace right here in my purse." She patted her purse with her fingertips.

"You draw him out and I'll spray him till he'll cry for his momma."

Norma Sue bumped her with a hip. "Stop patting that thing. You want to alert this bozo that you've got something in that thing you call a purse. From the size of that suitcase you wouldn't be able to find the mace before he kidnapped Amber and hauled her off to who knows where."

"I can pat my purse if I want to and I can find it when I want to."

"Ladies," Adela said sweetly as she stepped in between them and Amber. "Focus. Tensions are high, hold it together. We are here to help Amber not fight over some mace."

Norma Sue looked alarmed. "Right. We're going down to see Lacy and Sheri. We'll talk to you in a bit." She winked and Amber was glad they were here but also glad to see them head toward the salon. She entered the dress store and a few minutes later she went into the candy store and visited with the ladies there. A little while later she came out with a bag of candy and stood right there on the sidewalk and ate a piece of caramel. Her phone rang. Her heart began running away as she tugged the phone from her purse. It was from Sadie.

Amber answered the call wanting very much to talk to her friend.

"Hey, Sadie, so good to hear from you." The phone line crackled with a bad connection but she could still make out Sadie's familiar voice. "How are Mr. and Mrs. Masterson doing?" she asked teasingly.

"We're doing wonderful. We've had the best week, oh so romantic..." the line crackled but the joy in Sadie's voice couldn't be denied.

"I can't wait to hear all about it."

"How are you? I've tried to not worry but I'm anxious to know if they've caught your stalker?"

Amber had started walking down the sidewalk toward Adela's boarding house. The phone lines were coming and going and she hoped to get a better signal but it wasn't improving. She also wasn't sure how much to reveal to Sadie at the moment. She was still technically on her honeymoon until she arrived at her front doorstep. Right? She just couldn't put a damper on that.

"It's going okay, Sadie. I'll tell you about it when you get home. How much longer?"

"We're not sure. We're stuck in traffic so it may be this evening before we get there." The connection nearly gave out.

"I can't wait to see you, and hear about everything." She just couldn't bring herself to tell Sadie that Ned was still lurking out there somewhere. Before she could say more the line died.

Pocketing the phone she halted on the sidewalk. To get to the older home at the end of the street she crossed over a small crossroad and then walked to the front porch of the old home that had been turned into apartments. This, she was told was where Adela had grown up as a child. It was a huge home with gingerbread trim, turrets and stained glass panes in the upper portions of some of the windows. The front porch wrapped around and invited one to sit and enjoy the day. She could imagine sitting on that swing with her beau and being courted.

She glanced around and felt as if she were being watched...which was silly since she knew she was being watched by any number of eyes. Those eyes were probably all wondering why she'd left the hub of town and isolated herself here at the edge of town. It wasn't the smartest thing to do but she'd been talking to Sadie and had just been drawn in this direction. Now, she wanted a closer look. She noticed there were several vehicles parked on the other side of the building in a shaded parking area. One of the trucks held furniture. Someone was moving in or out. There was an apartment for rent sign in the yard. As she walked up the steps the door opened and a young woman came out carrying a potted plant.

"Hi," Amber said. "Are you moving out?"

The young woman smiled. "I am. I'm all packed up I just need to put this plant in the truck and then lock the door and I'm done. Are you interested in renting? It's a great place."

"No, I'm not but..." she thought about that statement. "You know, now that I'm here, would you mind if I took a look at your apartment?"

"Oh not at all." She fished a key from her jeans pocket. "Matter of fact, if you want to look and then lock up when you're done you can just drop this into the key drop box on the inside of the door. Adela wouldn't mind I'm sure."

Amber took the key ring with two keys on it. "Thanks." She was shocked at the trust the woman was placing on her but then had to remind herself that she was not the city. This was Mule Hollow and she was realizing that this little town was safe. The danger that was lurking somewhere for her had been led here by her.

"Apartment 3B. Thanks," the woman said and then hurried down the steps to her truck.

Amber entered the historic home with its dark wood floors and staircase carved with intricate carvings on the railings. Excitement filled her and despite knowing she had just veered from the plan she headed up the creaking stairs.

She was on the top landing when she thought she heard a door open somewhere in the building...

Chase couldn't see Amber any longer. The woman had totally gone against what they'd discussed and instead of staying in the main area of town where he and Brady could watch her she'd headed off toward the apartment house. And she'd been talking on the phone.

Was she talking to Ned? His gut was feeling like a block of concrete as he eased from the vacant building beside Pete's Feed and Seed. Across the street the door of Heavenly Inspirations opened and an entire herd of women came outside. The group included the posse, Lacy and Sheri they all had baffled expressions. Esther Mae led the pack as they hustled across the street.

"Where did our girl go? We lost her."

He'd been on the opposite side of the street so had a better view to watch Amber. "She went to your apartment house, Adela."

"Oh, that's too far away."

There had been a barn fire at one of the ranches and Zane had had to respond to that and Brady had begun receiving calls that fences were cut all over the main roads. Herds of cattle had escaped causing havoc on the main roads into town. He'd called Chase and told him what was happening and that he had to respond. Chase was to call him the minute any sign of trouble started.

Ty and Dalton called to say fences were down and cattle were everywhere on their main rode too.

Chase knew Ned was here. And he'd caused this...

"Ladies, stay put."

Moving fast, he cut across the street and jogged down the alley taking the back way to the apartments. He had no way of knowing if she was okay or not but his gut was churning and every cell in his body was telling him something wasn't right.

Amber entered the apartment and smiled. It was dark wood floors and pale butter walls with dark wood trim. The apartment had an oval sitting area in the turret adding an extra layer of charm to the space. She moved to look around the corner at the small but neat kitchen and then she crossed the hardwood floors and entered the bedroom. It was decorated in much the same way as the living space with the dark wood floors and pale blue walls. She pushed open the bathroom door and spied the beautiful claw footed tub surrounded by white tile. There was so much about the apartment that she loved. The thought crossed her mind that she could live in this place.

She'd turned to go back into the bedroom when she gasped and dropped her phone. Ned Talbert stood in the doorway blocking her escape.

He looked angry. Wild eyes and unshaven. When he'd followed her before he'd been clean shaven and wearing business attire. Now his shirt was rumpled, dirty and he had a stubble on his jaw. He glared at her and she saw his fist clench.

Amber was trapped.

"I told you you'd be sorry. You took something of mine. Now I'm going to make you pay and take something of yours."

His words didn't really make sense. What of hers was he going to take?

Amber willed her heart rate to back down and breathed evenly as she strove to remain calm. She glanced around but she'd effectively trapped herself because she'd gotten distracted by the beauty of this apartment. What had she been thinking in the first place?

"You don't scare me," she said, despite the truth that yes, she was a little worried. Ned wasn't a small man but that didn't really matter, she could do this. Her mouth went dry when he pulled a gun from his jacket. That changed things up a bit.

He smirked. "You thought you could hide from me but you were wrong. When I want something I don't stop until I get it. Patricia was mine and you put ideas in her head and made her leave. I find that offensive. Now move," he waved the gun and stepped away from the doorway to let her walk through. "And if you bolt I'll shoot and I'm a very good marksman."

Amber complied moving into the front room. He followed close behind and poked the automatic into the small of her back. "Downstairs we're going hunting."

Uncertain where this was going she did as she was told. The stairs creaked with each step and her nerves were rattled when they reached the first floor. The door was opened and she walked out onto the beautiful porch. Getting shot here wasn't exactly what she'd envisioned when she'd first entered the building. Crazily she'd been toying with the idea of exploring new possibilities for her life. She was young. She could recoup and reevaluate if she made a change and didn't like it.

She had not been thinking...this.

When Chase stepped out from the back of the building and called out Ned's name she nearly fainted with fear. She glanced over her shoulder and saw Ned's unstable grin.

"Right on time. I told you I was going to take something of yours."

Amber gasped. He was going to shoot Chase.

"Let her go, Ned," Chase demanded.

"Chase," Amber called a warning but before she could process the word she almost anticipated Ned's move as the gun moved from the small of her back and aimed toward Chase.

Amber swung her arm up and kicked at the same instant. The gun exploded as she made contact with Ned's arm.

Ned stumbled back but she was looking at Chase. The bullet spun him, and knocked him to his knees and then he fell forward and hit the ground.

"Chase!" she screamed, and started for him. Ned slammed the gun against her temple knocking her to her knees, she was dazed. Ned grabbed her by the arm and hauled her to her feet, then drug her toward a car only a few feet away. He stuffed her inside as she tried to clear the fuzziness from her throbbing head. He climbed in behind the steering wheel and gunned the car as he pulled out of the parking lot. Amber's forehead was pressed against the glass and her dizzy eyes were focused on Chase...he hadn't moved from where he lay.

Amber shook her head. She could not pass out. She had to get back to Chase. She shook her head trying to rid it of the cobwebs as she forced herself to dive for the steering wheel.

They heard the gun go off and immediately everyone started moving. Norma Sue had been a ranch woman all her life and she'd handled her fair share of rustlers and rattlesnakes. Trouble had come calling to her quiet town and she didn't take kindly to it.

"Get back everyone," she bellowed and strode to her truck.

"Sheri, call Brady," Lacy yelled as she raced off the boardwalk and ran toward her beloved 1958 pink Cadillac convertible.

Norma had her truck door opened and was reaching inside as Esther Mae hustled from the boardwalk.

"Wait for me, Lacy!" the redhead screamed trotting behind the beauty operator. Sheri had her phone out and was dialing numbers as she followed Esther Mae. Lacy didn't bother to open her door but, instead hopped over the door and plopped into the seat as if she hadn't just had a baby a month ago. She fired up the engine as Esther Mae wrenched open the door and fell into the back seat. Sheri followed as Norma Sue pulled her double barrel shotgun from behind the seat and grabbed her box of shells. One never knew when a rattlesnake or a coyote was gonna come calling and she never went unprepared. She was standing in the middle of the road when Lacy gunned the caddy and backed out beside her. Yanking the door open Norma Sue hopped into the front seat shotgun propped on the armrest.

"Hang on girls let's roll," Lacy called.

"Be safe," Adela called. "I'll check on Chase."

Norma Sue knew if that boy was okay he'd

have already been in pursuit. So Adela was thinking straight—he probably needed her.

And Amber needed them.

They passed App and Stanley hustling to App's truck and Norma hoped they were going to follow.

"You're gonna have to step on it, Lace," Sheri called from the backseat.

Lacy shot her a look. "You got that gun loaded yet, Norma?"

Norma dropped two shells into the barrel and snapped the barrel in place. "Hit it, Lacy. You get me close enough and I'll blow his tires smooth off that car."

"Norma, don't you miss," Esther Mae yelled above the roar of the huge caddy engine as they all were pressed back against their seats the instant Lacy floored the gas pedal. They shot forward like a rocket.

CHAPTER NINETEEN

Chase brought himself to his knees blood dripped from his shoulder and pain seared through him. He had to get to Amber. He stumbled forward just as Adela came hustling around the corner of the apartments.

"Amber," he called staggering toward her. He had to get to his truck. Adela yanked her sweater from around her shoulders and pressed it to his wound.

"You have to stop the bleeding," she urged. "The girls have gone after Amber."

"The girls?" What craziness was this?

App's big old truck came wheeling into the parking lot and the old man hung his head out the window. Stanley was in the driver's seat and Sam jumped from the back seat and hurried to him and Adela.

"Come on, let's get you in the truck. Honey, get

on in thar we'll tend to this on the way. We got women to catch. No tellin' whose gonna get shot with that group flying across country."

Chase stumbled to the truck. Thinking he must be in worse shape than he thought from what he was hearing. He collapsed into the back seat and Adela immediately set to tying up his wound and stopping the bleeding. Sam climbed in behind him and slammed the door.

"Hang on," App yelled and wheeled the big truck around and swerved out of the parking lot.

"Who went after Amber?" he asked wincing when petite Adela nearly punched her tiny hand through the bullet hole attempting to stop the bleeding.

"Lacy's driving with Norma Sue and her shotgun riding shotgun," Stanley boomed. "Esther Mae and Sheri are with them too. In that caddy with Lacy driving they'll catch her. Don't you worry."

Worry? Chase started praying because this had just turned into a nightmare. He grabbed the back of the seat and sat up so he could focus on the road up ahead. He blinked and could see the hot pink caddy up ahead. Lacy's blonde hair whipped in the wind as she drove the car like she was racing in the Indy 500. "Can you make this truck go any faster, App?"

"Danged ole truck ain't got the juice it used to but hang on," he warned and punched the pedal to the floor.

Behind them, thank the good Lord, Chase heard sirens.

Amber had lunged toward the steering wheel and Ned had aimed the gun at her. Now she sat in the seat willing her head to stop spinning. Blood trickled down her forehead from where he'd hit her and she figured she had a concussion, it was throbbing something fierce. But if she could just get him stopped she might be able to get away. Fear for Chase clung to her and she had to get back to him. Had to check on him. She glanced over her shoulder and almost choked...

The *posse* was in pursuit.

There was no mistaking Lacy's caddy hurling toward them in hot pursuit and Lacy's trademark white blonde hair whipping in the wind. And behind her, the unmistakable red hair of Esther Mae stood straight up in the wind. As the car gained she could make out Sheri beside Esther

Mae and in the passenger's seat there sat Norma Sue and...Amber squinted—the ranch woman had a double barrel shotgun pointed straight at them.

Amber had just enough time to brace as fire erupted from the end of the gun and the next thing she knew the rear tire of Ned's car blew.

Ned cursed beside her and Amber dove toward the steering wheel. Just as his pistol went off.

Chase watched in horror as Norma Sue aimed and shot the rear tire nearly smooth off the car that had Amber inside. The car swerved and then, it did a wild spin and caught two tires. He prayed it wouldn't flip. Because he knew there was no way Amber had on a seatbelt.

The wheels came back down, but the car spun several times then veered off the road and slammed into a ditch. App screeched to a halt right behind Lacy. Chaos erupted as he made it out of the car and yelled for everyone to get back. "He's armed and dangerous."

Thankfully they all moved away as he crouched down and moved to the back of the car. There was no movement inside. Brady and Zane screeched to a halt and within minutes they'd had the doors opened. Ned lay motionless. Chase got to Amber's side and pulled the door open. The bag had hit her too but she was only stunned. She gasped when she saw him and launched herself from the car.

"You're alive," she cried and clung to him.

He clung to her and buried his face in her hair. "I thought I'd lost you," he said.

She shook her head. "Never."

She looked up at him. Tears in her eyes. "He told me he was going to take something I loved. And that was you."

Chase went still. "You love me?"

"Oh, Chase, I do. Crazy I know but all I could think about was you. I knew I'd do anything to get back to you."

He smiled and pulled her close. "I love you too crazy girl." And then he kissed her.

"Okay you two, love birds into the truck. Someone call the ambulance," Brady demanded as he steered them toward his truck. "We've got a concussion and a lot of lost blood going on here."

Amber looked dazed. "Maybe true. But I do love you, Chase Hartley."

He grinned. She did look like she might not be thinking straight. He sank to the seat of Brady's truck and wrapped his good arm tightly around

Amber and then…everything went black.

Amber looked around the apartment at Adela's as the women all crowded into the living room. This was her guardian angel group. The posse plus some. Sure-shot Norma Sue, speed racer Lacy, fearless Esther Mae, Sheri and Adela. Sadie and Maddie were here too and looking at all of them Amber had to blink back tears. Never in her entire life had she felt such a sweet sisterhood as she did now, with this group. They'd come after her. Risked themselves to stop a madman from harming her. And there had been all the others too. App and Stanley, Sam, Brady and Zane. And there had been Chase.

She sniffed and wiped a tear as they all had pitched in to on the apartment project-all but Chase who had no clue what she was up to. Ned Talbert was in jail now and would be for a very long time. It had taken two weeks for her to feel normal again. She thought her head might never stop swimming or the headaches go away that were left over from the severe concussion that Ned had given her when he'd smacked her with his pistol, but they finally had.

She'd said some crazy things when she'd been fuzzy in the brain and one of those things had been telling Chase that she loved him.

But he'd told her the same thing. He'd lost a lot of blood and by the time the ambulance had arrived they'd both passed out. When they'd awakened they'd each drawn back a little, she figured he'd realized the craziness to his declaration and she'd known that hers had been completely unlike her. She'd reminded herself that she needed to be cautious. Falling in love in a week...it was irrational. And she and Chase were both rational people. They thought things out. They planned. They did not give into irrational things.

So they'd not said the L words again. They'd talked. And he'd even kissed her and told her he wanted her to stay. He'd even told her either way that he was coming to court her and that she needed to be ready...but she hadn't been able to think straight and she'd made no promises. This was too important. She'd had to think.

"So, what do you think?"

Sadie beamed. "I think it's a wonderful idea. And after all you've been through I believe you're making a very smart choice."

"I agree. This apartment is perfect for you," Maddie said.

"I think it's great," Esther Mae huffed, "but I still don't understand. You two are perfect for each other and this just does not make sense to me."

"Esther Mae, hush," Norma Sue snapped. "Give the girl some room. She's been through one heck of an ordeal."

"I know it. I was there too, remember. I nearly passed smooth out when you shot that tire out and sent that car into conniption fits."

"We all did," Lacy said. "But now these two have a shot let's give them space." She winked. "You go, girl."

Amber watched as Lacy and Sadie hustled everyone toward the door. Feeling both trepidation and elation at the same time. "Wish me luck," she called.

Sadie halted and glared at her. "You don't need luck. God's got this and after all that happened...everything that could have gone wrong already did."

"Ain't that the truth," harrumphed Norma Sue as she reached the stairs and led the procession down and out of the building.

Amber listened to their footsteps and chatter

disappear and she took a deep breath as she looked around once more. She'd moved a few things in from her apartment back in Houston. The rest would come later. But already the apartment was taking shape. Tonight would be her first night to sleep in her new home. Tomorrow she would celebrate Thanksgiving Day with Sadie and Rafe and hopefully Chase.

She heard the rumble of a truck and went to the window and peered out. Chase shut the door of his truck and stared at the building. He looked tired. She hadn't seen him in several days and though he'd called, she hadn't answered the calls because she needed him to have his space. She needed him not to feel responsible for her.

Adela had asked him to come by the apartment for a moment. He was probably wondering why she needed him to stop by.

Walking to the top of the stairs Amber waited for him to come through the doors and see the note telling him to come upstairs. When he looked up he stopped.

"Amber," he said. "What are you doing here?"

He looked so wonderful. If he just didn't look so tired she'd say he was doing great but she had a feeling he wasn't sleeping good.

She smiled at him, knowing her heart knew what it wanted. "I have a surprise and I'm hoping you like it."

He moved up the steps, his gaze steady on hers as he came. "This building doesn't give you bad memories?"

She shook her head. "No. It's not this gorgeous old home's fault about what happened here. And actually, what happened here was good in many ways."

He reached the landing where she stood and her heart was pounding so hard it was a wonder he couldn't hear it. She stared at him, drinking him in and knowing she could look at him for the rest of her life.

It had been a month now that they'd known each other so that wasn't as off the wall as a week.

"Are you alright?" he asked. Touching her cheek with his palm.

"I'm good. Just happy you're alive and well." She reached for his hand. "Follow me please I need to talk to you."

She led him through the doorway and into her new home. He paused just inside the room. Looking around. "Amber?"

She laughed. "Chase?"

"What are you up to?" he asked.

"Welcome to my new home."

"You're moving here?"

She nodded and moved to stand beside him. "Chase, I know we're both practical, rational people. And I know that we went through a week together that was kind of intense...but, when you were shot. When I thought I'd lost you I really did know that I loved you. I haven't said it again because I didn't want to scare you away. But it's true. I decided to start over here in Mule Hollow. I've taken that job at No Place Like Home. I want to see the results of what I've always done. I want to live near you. I know what I feel for you is love...but it's happened so fast and I'm worried that it might be too fast for you after all. So, no pressure on you. I just wanted to start here and see if you might want to—" her words stumbled to a halt when he smiled, a slow sexy smile that sent butterflies swooning inside of her.

"Amber, darlin', I told you I loved you the day Ned tried to kill us. And my mind hasn't changed. I've just pulled back to give you some space because I knew you had a lot on your mind. You've been under tremendous pressure and I wanted you to have time to process us."

Relief filled her. "Us. I like us."

He pulled her into his arms. "I love us," he said and kissed her so she knew he really, really loved "us". When he pulled back her knees were weak.

"Oh," she sighed. "I could get used to that."

He grinned. "God gave us a second chance when I could have lost you that day and I'm forever grateful. I'd planned to come to Houston and court you if that's what it took. Because you deserve to be courted. And that's what's going to happen. You're going to live here. Get settled into your new job and your new town and I'm going to take you to dinner, take you to the movies, on picnics."

"On horseback rides," she interjected.

"On horseback rides too," he said. "I'm going to take my time, and make sure you feel just as cherished as you're supposed to feel. And then, Amber Rivers, if you still want me, then I'm going to marry you. How does that sound?"

Amber knew what he was doing. He was showing her that he would be around. That he cared enough to spend time with her and be there for her. He just didn't realize that she already knew that about him.

She wrapped her arms around his neck and

pulled his lips to hers. "I think that sounds wonderful. Just as long as you're going to marry me. Because I'm planning on marrying you and last I heard it takes two to make that work."

He chuckled. "You are so right about that." And then he kissed her and she decided that life in the country was going to be far, far, far from boring like she'd once believed.

—The End—

Dear Readers:

I hope you enjoyed Chase and Amber's story as much as I loved creating it! CHASE (#3) of the New Horizon/Mule Hollow series was a blast to write and the first 5 books of this series are now available: HER MULE HOLLOW COWBOY (#1) RAFE (#2) CHASE (#3) TY (#4) DALTON (#5) and then TREB (#6). To be notified of new releases *and* all other news on my books, sign up for my NEWSLETTER today at:

> http://debraclopton.com/contest/

I'll be starting a Review "Posse" soon and would love to have you join…more on that soon! For now, if you'd consider leaving a review of this book I will be YOUR fan forever ☺ xoxo

Happy Reading!
Debra

New Horizon Ranch: Mule Hollow Series

Her Mule Hollow Cowboy (Book 1)

Five ranch-hands inherit a Texas ranch from their boss. These cowboys and cowgirl vow to honor their beloved boss by making the New Horizon Ranch the success he envisioned when he chose to leave his legacy in their care. Along the way they each find the love of a lifetime. You'll fall in love with these fun, sweet, emotional love stories.

Cowboy Cliff Masterson saw a woman in need and stepped in—because Maddie was too stubborn to ask...

Cowgirl Maddie Rose has never belonged anywhere but she's just inherited part of New Horizon Ranch—along with her partners, four handsome, extremely capable cowboys... Maddie's trying to adjust to her new life and her new partners she's still unable to believe she's an owner of this fabulous ranch. Not sure why she was included, she's out to prove herself worthy of the honor of the inheritance. Loving her new life in the small Texas town of Mule Hollow, she's determined that, for the first time in her life, she's going to finally belong somewhere...

Professional Bull Rider Cliff Masterson has been chasing his dreams for years—or has he been running from his past? He's searching for more in life and ready to dig in his spurs and put down roots deep in the heart of Texas. Rescuing a beautiful cowgirl from being trampled by a bull has him dreaming of romance, home and hearth.

But Maddie's had enough people in her life leave and she's not willing to risk her heart on him—Sparks fly as he's determined to prove to the feisty cowgirl that the only think he's chasing now is wedding bells with her…

Can the Matchmakin' Posse of Mule Hollow help this couple find their happily ever after?

Rafe (Book 2)

When runaway bride, Sadie Archer's car breaks down on the outskirts of Mule Hollow, Texas, she's not exactly dressed to fix the blown tire. Then again, she hadn't planned on this road trip or her life falling apart a week before her wedding. But now that she's hit the road, destination unknown, Sadie's decided it's time to disappear for a while and find out exactly what it is she wants out of life. But first she needs to change her flat tire and that is easier said than done when one is wearing…

A bunny suit!

Ex-cowboy star Rafe Masterson thinks he's seeing things at first but yes—that is definitely a female head sticking out of the furry white bunny suit, tangling with a spare tire. A cowboy who guards his heart carefully, he's still always willing to help someone in need…even one wearing white fur from top to bottom. Completely captivated by the unusual woman, Rafe senses she's in trouble in more ways than the flat tire. He's part owner of the New Horizon Ranch and offers her a job as cook—even though they don't need a cook.

Sadie accepts even though she can't really cook but this is the perfect answer to her needs right now…and how hard can it be anyway?

These two might be down-on-love but love hasn't given up on them and the Matchmaking Posse of Mule Hollow has just gotten them in their sights…

Chase (Book 3)

Being a bridesmaid at her best friend's wedding in the sleepy town of Mule Hollow Texas is the perfect place for Amber Rivers to lay low to avoid a stalker hot on her heels back in Houston. She loves her job and her city life and isn't looking to stay long in the country-but she's blindsided by her attraction to the self-assured rancher, Chase

Hartley…

Chase agrees to watch over socialite Amber while his partner heads off on his honeymoon but despite the high voltage sparks lighting up between them he has no intention of getting any closer to Amber than necessary to keep her safe. But he soon realizes there's a whole lot more to Amber than he first assumed and keeping his distance is becoming harder with every passing moment they're together.

An outside threat plus a little friendly tampering from the meddling Matchmakin' Posse of Mule Hollow puts this couple on high alert as they try not to fall in love.

Ty (Book 4)

Best friends forever…happily ever that is…Christmas wedding bells will be ringing if the Matchmakin' Posse of Mule Hollow can get this stubborn cowboy and cowgirl together under the mistletoe for the most anticipated kiss of the holiday.

Will Ty Calder, mild mannered partner in the New Horizon Ranch, get his secret Christmas wish and heal his lonesome heart this season? Find out in Book 4 of the New Horizon Ranch/Mule Hollow series.

Horse trainer Ty Calder did the right thing four

years ago and sent his best friend, Mia Shaw off with a hug and best wishes in her quest for her rodeo dreams to come true. But now she's back for the Christmas holiday and he's not sure he can send her off again without revealing his true feelings…

Mia is back in Mule Hollow healing up from an injury that could end her run for the championship. But, lately her heart's not been completely committed to her rodeo dreams and Ty has her thinking he might just be the reason.

Suddenly, tensions are running high between Mia and Ty…sparks are flying and have been spotted by the Matchmakin' Posse. Now these two are dodging mistletoe, matchmakers and the kiss they're both fighting to avoid and longing for.

But Ty can't believe Mia is ready to give up on her dreams when she's so close…he knows it means more to her than most people realize. No matter how much he wants a life with Mia he refuses to stand in the way of her dreams even if it means losing her forever…

It may take his four partners at the New Horizon Ranch and the town of Mule Hollow to get these two believing Christmas is especially the time that love can conquer all.

This is going to be one Christmas these two will remember forever…

Dalton (Book 5)

Dalton Borne is a cowboy who keeps his past closed up inside. He's watched his partners at the New Horizon Ranch find love and he's happy for them and even envious. But his past prevents him from believing he deserves a future that includes a love of his own. But then one stormy night he rescues a very pregnant Rae Anne Tyson from floodwaters and ends up delivering her baby on the side of the road. Suddenly Dalton's life is turned upside down and no matter what he believes he does or doesn't deserve—he can't walk away from helping Rae Anne.

Don't miss book 5 in the New Horizon Ranch series…Dalton Borne is one Texas cowboy you'll never forget.

Treb (Book 6)

Former special ops soldier Treb Carson has returned to his ranching roots joining up with the New Horizon Ranch. Afghanistan and the loss of his brother have him ready to move forward into happier times-he's looking for love and to start a family. He's not expecting to be captivated by Megan Tanner, the completely wrong woman for his plans. The workaholic, new veterinarian in town doesn't have marriage on her agenda and she's made that clear, but he can't get her or the kiss they share off his mind.

Megan Tanner has her personal reasons for not believing in happily-ever-after, but now she's moved to the hometown of the Matchmakin' Posse of Mule Hollow. Avoiding their antics is easy for now, its calving season and that means no time for anything but work and building her vet practice. But then she's blindsided by the smokin'-hot, ex-military cowboy and the immediate sparks she can't deny or the kiss she can't forget.

Treb knows all the reasons why Megan isn't the woman for him…but he can't seem to stop himself. Now he's determined to find out why Megan is so against falling in love and proving to her that she can trust him with her heart.

And he's got a certain three, nosy ladies on his side…can the "Posse" help this couple find their happily-ever-after?

Sign up for Debra Clopton's Newsletter to find out about future books as soon as they're released! http://debraclopton.com/contest/

More Books by Debra Clopton

Mule Hollow Matchmakers Series
The Trouble with Lacy Brown (Book 1)
And Baby Makes Five (Book 2)

The Men of Mule Hollow Series
Her Forever Cowboy (Book 1)
Cowboy for Keeps (Book 2)
Yuletide Cowboy (Book 3)

The Cowboys of Sunrise Ranch
Her Unforgettable Cowboy (Book 1)
Her Unexpected Cowboy (Book 2)
Her Unlikely Cowboy (Book 3)

For the complete list, visit her website
www.debraclopton.com

Made in the USA
Middletown, DE
10 April 2017